Deadly Intentions

Blackmoore Sisters Cozy Mystery Book 5

Leighann Dobbs

This is a work of fiction.

None of it is real. All names, places, and events are products of the author's imagination. Any resemblance to real names, places, or events are purely coincidental, and should not be construed as being real.

Deadly Intentions
Copyright © 2014
Leighann Dobbs
http://www.leighanndobbs.com
All Rights Reserved.

No part of this work may be used or reproduced in any manner, except as allowable under "fair use," without the express written permission of the author.

Cover art by: http://www.coverkicks.com

To my father:
Frank J. Trabucco
January 17, 1931 - April 29, 2014
You had a good run.

Chapter One

Jolene Blackmoore had always known there was something suspicious about her mother's death. She'd tried to say so at the time, but no one had listened seven years ago.

Back then, she'd been only fourteen ... and who listened to a hormone-riddled, grief-stricken teenager?

No one.

But, now she was twenty-one with a private investigator's license and the knowledge and skills that went with it. It was time to prove what she'd always known.

She stared at the pictures on her computer screen, which she'd downloaded from the Noquitt Police Department database. It had been surprisingly easy to hack into.

Okay, so it wasn't quite legal, she thought, *but if they really didn't want people in there, they should make the password a bit more secure.*

The file on Johanna Blackmoore's death was sorely lacking in information.

There had been just one witness who claimed to have seen Johanna fling herself over the cliff— Earl Whiting. The report stated that Earl had been out lobstering in his boat off the point that evening and had seen Johanna on the edge of the cliff, alone.

According to Earl, she 'looked up to the heavens then threw herself off'. Too bad Earl was known to spend most of his days drinking. He wasn't what Jolene would call a reliable witness.

It looked like the whole investigation had been a sham from the start, just as she'd suspected. Even at her young age, she'd been able to tell they weren't doing a good job, but when she'd tried to voice her objections, the new sheriff in town, Sheriff Overton, had brushed her off, saying that she was just an emotional child.

Overton hadn't liked anyone questioning his methods and paid her back by constantly dogging her throughout the rest of her teenage years, threatening to arrest her for any slight violation and making life as miserable as he could for her and her sisters every chance he got. She'd always had the distinct impression that Overton had bungled the investigation on purpose.

Needless to say, she'd been rather pleased when Overton mysteriously disappeared from town last summer. *Good riddance*, she thought.

"Meow."

The family cat, Belladonna, jumped up on the table, stepping lightly on the keyboard and standing right in front of the screen. She turned her pale blue eyes on Jolene, who sighed and reached out to pull the cat into her lap.

"What's the matter, can't find any mice to torture?" Jolene stroked that cat's silky white fur affectionately as she stared at the pictures on the screen—pictures of the cliff her mother had jumped from seven years ago.

The cliff sat on the edge of their property. In fact, she could see it pretty well from the the room she was sitting in right now.

Her eyes drifted over to the large window. Outside, the view of the Atlantic Ocean was usually stunning. Today, gray clouds hovered over the dark, stormy seas. Rain beat against the window, obscuring her view, but she could still make out the edge of the cliff.

The very same cliff from which her mother had jumped seven years ago, smashing on the rocks thirty feet below before being swept into the sea.

Jolene's fingers stole up to the silver heart shaped locket she wore around her neck. She'd discovered the locket in an old suitcase she'd used to take on an assignment she and her sisters had gone on out west. As soon as she'd seen the locket, she felt an immediate connection. It wasn't until later that she found out it looked exactly like the one her mother had always worn.

Jolene guessed her subconscious must have recognized it, even though she didn't consciously remember it as her mother's locket. She'd been too self-absorbed at fourteen to think much about what jewelry other people wore, but she'd been told her mother never took that locket off.

So, the locket she'd found couldn't possibly be her mother's. It didn't have any pictures inside and the design wasn't that uncommon—she'd researched it—so it must be just a strange coincidence.

Too bad Jolene didn't believe in coincidences.

Belladonna reached a pink paw up and batted at the locket.

"You don't think it's a coincidence either, do you?" Jolene asked the cat, who answered her by settling into her lap and purring loudly.

But the locket *couldn't* be her mother's, because she would have been wearing it when she jumped. And if that were the case, it would have smashed to bits on the rock, and those bits would have fallen into the ocean. Unless she hadn't been wearing it that day ... or someone had taken it from her before she fell.

Jolene shuddered at the thought of her mother's slim body plummeting down the steep cliff. She could almost hear the sickening crunch of her hitting the jagged rocks below.

She couldn't imagine why anyone would do that to themselves, especially not her mother, who she remembered as being perpetually cheerful and happy.

Everyone had said the premature death of Johanna's husband, their father, years before had worn her down. She'd been depressed and finally couldn't go on. But Jolene didn't remember her that way. Naturally they'd all been devastated when their father died, but Johanna had bravely soldiered on. It had brought her even closer to her daughters. Jolene felt certain her mother would never have left them alone like that ... not unless she was forced to.

Or maybe Jolene had just been too absorbed in herself to notice how her mother had been hurting.

Jolene leaned forward, dislodging the cat from her lap. She clicked the mouse, flipping from picture to picture.

There has to be something here in these pictures ... some kind of clue.

Belladonna stretched and let out a tiny 'meow', then stepped back onto the table blocking the screen once again.

"Shoo." Jolene wrestled the resistant cat out of the way.

In the struggle, Belladonna's paws pushed down on the keyboard, pressing keys at random. The cat jumped down from the table and Jolene looked back at the computer screen. Apparently, Belladonna had pressed the right combination of keys to enlarge the picture. Jolene fiddled with the keyboard, trying to put the screen back to normal size.

Then something in the picture caught her eye. Jolene squinted at the picture on the screen that showed the edge of the cliff where the grass ended and there was just bare dirt. This was the exact place where her mother supposedly stood before jumping thirty feet to the ocean below. All accounts said her mother had been alone on the cliff that night.

But if the accounts were true and her mother *had* been alone ... why were there men's shoe prints in the dirt?

***

The sound of laughter drifted down the hall, announcing the arrival of her sisters and pulling Jolene from her thoughts. She clicked off the screen before they could see what she was doing. She didn't want them to know she was looking into their mother's death until she had something more to go on. No sense in stirring up those painful memories until there was a solid reason.

"Working this late?" Fiona frowned at Jolene. "You should take some time to relax."

Jolene's heart warmed at her sister's concern. Fiona was the second oldest, and she and the oldest sister, Morgan, had taken over the job of mothering Jolene after Johanna had died. Celeste, the sister in between Jolene and Fiona had been barely eighteen when Johanna died and, even though she'd helped keep Jolene on track, she was much more relaxed about it than the older sisters. Jolene was an adult now, but old habits are hard to break and the two older sisters still looked after her like mother hens.

"I will. I was just finishing up some research on the case Jake has me working on," Jolene said, referring to Fiona's boyfriend, Jake Cooper. Fiona's eyes lit up at the mention of the former member of the Noquitt police department who'd turned in his badge last summer to open his own private detective agency. He'd hired Jolene as his assistant when she'd shown an uncanny aptitude for police work, computer forensics in particular.

"What's the case about?" Celeste rubbed her hands through her short-cropped, blonde hair as she glanced out the window at the quickly darkening sky. The sun had a few hours longer before it would set, but the dark clouds made it seem like night had fallen already.

"Jebediah Powers hired us to prove that Gordon Ellis fooled with his lobstering traps."

"That old feud again?" Morgan made a face. "Those two have been feuding for over twenty years."

"It's funny. The feud has been going on so long, no one even knows what started it." Fiona plopped into an oversized, white linen slipcovered chair and Morgan sat on the matching couch, pulling her long, silky jet-black hair over one shoulder as she settled back.

This was the girls' favorite room—the one they were most comfortable in. It had been their mother's favorite too. Jolene could see her influence everywhere, from the muted blues and grays to the overstuffed furniture to the seaside accents. Her heart tugged, remembering the care her mother had put into decorating the room.

"So, how are things at *Sticks and Stones*?" Jolene asked about the shop Morgan and Fiona ran together mostly to distract herself from thinking about Johanna.

"Great," Morgan said. "We're getting more and more customers traveling from all over the place. Not just people here on vacation."

"Word is getting out about how powerful Morgan's herbal remedies are," Fiona added.

"Not just the remedies," Celeste cut in, "I've heard more than one person talking about your healing gemstone jewelry and how it helped them with certain problems. You guys are getting quite a reputation."

The sisters ran *Sticks and Stones* from an old cottage located just outside the main part of town. They sold herbal remedies and healing crystals. It was no surprise that business was booming. The healing herbs and stones the girls made were more powerful than any ordinary herbs and stones because Morgan and Fiona had a special way with energy that enhanced the power of the herbs and stones. And they weren't the only ones in the family who had special powers.

All four of the girls had discovered they had what they called 'gifts' over the past two years. It had come on slowly at first, but over time, they had developed them so they could control them better.

Jolene frowned slightly. Was it strange the four sisters shared paranormal powers? Maybe it was a family trait like the ice-blue eyes that each of them had in common? Had their mother had special 'gifts', too? Jolene didn't remember anything like that, but then again most people with 'gifts' didn't talk about them much. She knew she and her sisters tried to keep their odd powers a secret. Maybe her mother had, too.

"Anyway, I'm glad I caught you all home tonight," Morgan reached into the back pocket of her jeans and pulled out a piece of lavender-colored paper. "I got this letter in the mail today. It's from Aunt Eliza."

"Aunt Eliza?" Fiona's long red curls fell over her shoulder as she leaned over the arm of the chair to take the paper from Morgan. "Jeez, I barely remember her."

"I don't remember her at all." Jolene eyed the letter Fiona was reading. The thick paper looked expensive. The writing was neat and orderly. "Who sends letters these days, anyway?"

"You were just a baby the last time we saw her." Fiona passed the letter over to Celeste. "She was Dad's younger sister, but I think there was some sort of falling out and they stopped talking to each other."

"It says here she's coming to Noquitt for a visit." Celeste tapped the paper.

"I know," Morgan said. "I was thinking we should invite her to stay here. After all, this was her home, once."

"Oh, yeah," Celeste passed the letter to Jolene. "I guess I forgot that Dad's family lived here before we did."

The centuries old house had been home to generations of Blackmoore's. Originally built by Isaiah Blackmoore three-hundred years earlier, it sat on a point of land situated at the mouth of Perkins Cove with the Atlantic Ocean on one side and the channel leading to the cove on the other.

The house had been modified and added to over the years, but a Blackmoore family had always lived there, including Jolene's family along with their grandmother, who had passed away years ago.

And now it was just her and her sisters.

It was hard to imagine her father as a little boy, running around the big mansion with his sister, not to mention the countless other generations that had lived there before them. If the house could only talk, Jolene was sure it would have some stories to tell.

She looked down at the letter in her hand. A chocolate brown curl fell in front of her face and she brushed it away absently as she studied the words in dark purple ink that looked almost like they had come from a fountain pen. The scent of lavender wafted up from the paper.

She got the distinct impression that even though she didn't remember Eliza Blackmoore from her youth, the woman was going to be someone she would never forget.

"So, what do you guys say?" Morgan prompted. "Should we ask her to stay with us?"

"Sure," Fiona said. "As long as no one else objects, I don't see why not."

"Yeah, it could be fun getting to know her better. I mean we really didn't know her well as kids. She was a lot younger than Dad, wasn't she?" Celeste asked.

"Yes, as I recall she was. I think she's only in her early forties. We have so few relatives now that I think it will be fun to have another Blackmoore to connect with." Morgan turned to Jolene who was still staring down at the letter. "Don't you agree, Jolene?"

"Huh?" Jolene looked up. "Oh, yes, of course. Invite her here for as long as she wants to stay. I don't see any phone number or email address to contact her, though. Did the envelope have a return address?"

"No," Morgan frowned. "That's the strange thing. It wasn't even postmarked. I just opened the mailbox and there it was."

"So how will we let her know she can stay here?" Fiona asked. "I wouldn't want her to book a hotel and lose her deposit."

Morgan shrugged. "I guess the only way is to tell her when she gets here."

"And when is that?" Celeste asked.

"Tomorrow."

"Meow!" Belladonna wailed just as a blinding flash of light lit up the sky outside the widow. Two seconds later, the thunderous boom had them all jumping out of their seats. The lights flickered, but stayed on.

Jolene's heart thudded in her chest as the four sisters exchanged nervous looks. It was early summer and thunderstorms certainly weren't unusual. The girls had weathered plenty of them in this house before. Jolene just hoped *this* storm wasn't a harbinger of things to come.

Chapter Two

Celeste Blackmoore woke to the warm rays of the sun on her face. She squinted one eye open and looked directly out her window at the glowing yellow ball rising out of the ocean. Last night's storm had passed and it looked like today was going to be a beauty.

She kicked the covers off, slid out of bed and stretched her slim, muscular body. Turning toward her closet, she rooted around in the pile of clothes on the floor for a pair of yoga pants she could wear down to the kitchen for her morning wheat grass drink before showering and heading off to the studio where she taught yoga and meditation.

"Looks like it's going to be a corker today."

Celeste's heart leaped into her throat. She whirled toward the voice, then relaxed as she recognized the misty figure swirling in the corner. She should be used to this by now.

"Morning, Grandma," Celeste said.

The mist swirled around and then manifested into a see-through version of Celeste's grandmother.

"Morning, dear." She turned to the window. "I do so miss these summer sunrises."

"Sorry."

"Oh nothing to be sorry about." Grandma turned from the window, a big smile on her face. "It's much nicer on the other side, anyway."

"Well, I'm in no hurry to find *that* out."

"No doubt. I hear you'll be having a visitor."

"You mean Aunt Eliza?"

"Yes." Grandma's face took on a pinched look. "My youngest. She was a surprise, you know. Always so headstrong. I never forgave myself for the falling out we had. She took off and that was the last I saw of her."

"I'm sorry. I never thought about it that way." Celeste felt a pang of sorrow for both her grandmother and her aunt. "She never contacted you or my father over all those years?"

"No, but don't let that color your perception of her. You'll like her. You have a lot in common."

"You mean she sees ghosts?"

Grandma laughed. "No. You're the only Blackmoore whose gifts manifest themselves in that way, as far as I know. I just think you girls will get along with her and I'm glad you're inviting her to stay here."

"Well, it is her house, too, I guess."

"That's the spirit! Oh, and one last thing ... the key is in the locket."

"Key? What key?" Celeste narrowed her eyes at her grandmother.

"Well, that's enough chit chat ... I really must be going." Grandma's ghost waved her hand dismissively, the charms on her bracelet swaying to and fro as she evaporated, leaving Celeste staring at an errant swirl of condensation drifting to the floor.

Leave it to Grandma to be so vague, Celeste shrugged, then turned back to the pile. Like her sisters, Celeste had been blessed with paranormal abilities. Her 'gift' was that she saw ghosts. She was used to her grandmother and sometimes other ghosts appearing and talking in vague terms, so she couldn't put too much stock in what her grandmother had said. But she did have empathy for the way the woman was obviously sad about what happened between her and Eliza.

Celeste felt a pang of sadness for Eliza, too. She didn't know what had happened to drive her from the family, but she imagined the woman must have been lonely all these years. Maybe Celeste and her sisters could make up for some of that.

Slipping on her yoga pants, Celeste ruffled her blonde hair so it spiked up on her head and headed down to the kitchen, vowing to do her best to make Eliza feel like a welcome part of the family.

***

Jolene stared into the mug of black coffee while she waited for the caffeine to wake up her brain.

"Morning, sleepyhead!" Celeste's chipper voice grated on her from the kitchen door.

"Mornin'," Jolene grumbled.

She watched as Celeste practically skipped over to the fridge, taking out some spinach, an avocado and coconut milk, then trotting it over to the counter where some green grass was growing in a container. Snipping off a large section of the grass, she threw everything enthusiastically into the blender.

Jolene took another sip of coffee and tried not to gag at the sight of the thick green goo swirling around in the blender. She hoped Celeste didn't spill any on the white marble counters—marble was porous and that goop would leave a stain.

"I talked to grandma this morning," Celeste chirped.

"Oh, really?" Jolene never knew what to say to that. Should she ask how their grandmother was, or was that inappropriate when it came to ghosts?

Celeste switched off the blender and poured the goo into a glass. "It seemed like she was really sad about the way things ended with Eliza and I got to thinking how lonely things must have been for our aunt ... you know, not seeing the family and all."

Jolene took another sip of coffee. She hadn't thought about it, but Celeste had a point.

"So I was thinking we should do our best to make her feel like family," Celeste continued.

"Okay. Sure. I mean I guess we would do that anyway, right?" Jolene asked.

"Yeah, but I was just thinking we could all make an extra effort." Celeste gulped down the juice. "Where is everyone else?"

"Morgan's out in the herb garden," Jolene thrust her chin in the direction of the window where Morgan could be seen bent over a row of seedlings she'd planted a few weeks ago. "Fiona must still be asleep. I haven't seen her yet this morning."

"Late night out with Jake?" Celeste wiggled her eyebrows up and down.

Jolene laughed—a sure sign the caffeine was kicking in. "Probably. Which reminds me. I'd better get going and work on that case before he fires me."

She sucked down the rest of her coffee, then slipped off the stool and put the coffee mug in the dishwasher before heading out the front door.

***

Jolene and Jake's office was a stuffy two-room suite on the second floor of a one-hundred-and-fifty year-old house that had been converted for commercial use. The first floor held the *Bagel Cafe*. As usual, the smell of fresh baked bagels made Jolene's stomach grumble, so she stopped there first.

Then, armed with a bag of bagels and two coffees, she climbed the creaky narrow stairs to the second floor. At the top, an oak door announced their office. 'Cooper Investigations' was stenciled on the frosted glass window in old fashioned gold and black lettering. She balanced the coffees, bagels and her large tote as she pushed the door open.

The outer room was empty. Jake was optimistic that a receptionist might sit out there one day. Jolene had a sneaking suspicion he had originally planned for her to do the receptionist tasks, but she had nipped that in the bud early on. She was a good investigator and her talents were better put to use in the field.

There were two desks in the inner room, which, thankfully, was quite large. Jake sat behind one of them, a large antique mahogany piece they'd liberated from Jolene's attic.

He looked up at her, his face freshly shaven and a twinkle in his gray eyes. Probably put there by Fiona, Jolene thought. He made a show of glancing at his watch.

"Thanks for coming to work today," he teased. They had a great relationship and even though Jake had only been her sister's boyfriend for a couple of years, he was like a big brother to her.

Jolene put one of the coffees on his desk and slid it toward him.

"Looks like you just got in yourself. Late night with my sister?" she teased him back, stifling a giggle when she saw a blush creep up his neck. Jake was a good guy. Fiona could do a lot worse.

She smiled, remembering how he had helped the sisters out when he first came to town. Morgan had been accused of murder, and Jake, who had just joined the Noquitt Police force after a career as a detective in Boston, had gone against Sheriff Overton to help them prove her innocence.

Going against Overton hadn't helped his standing down at the police station and Jake had eventually resigned from the force to start the private investigation business and taken Jolene under his wing.

The two of them had been pretty successful at it, too. Of course, her photographic memory and special gift of reading people's auras didn't hurt.

Jake peeled back the plastic tab on his coffee and took a sip.

"Did you bring me breakfast?" he asked, eyeing the *Bagel Cafe* bag.

"Yep. Your favorite." She opened the bag and angled it toward him, revealing a plump pumpernickel bagel on top.

Jake grabbed the bagel along with one of the small cream cheese containers. "Thanks."

"Welcome. Jeez, it's stuffy in here." That was one thing about the second floor of an old house; it got mighty hot, especially in summer. Jolene pushed open the old wooden window to let in some air.

From the second floor, she could see a tiny sliver of the ocean a quarter of a mile away. A cool breeze, fresh with salty sea air, wafted in through the window. Jolene could hear the cry of seagulls as she slid behind the green metal teacher's desk they'd gotten for free after the school renovation.

"So, what's up for today?" She bit into her poppy seed bagel.

"I was hoping you could follow Gail Flint this morning."

Jolene's brows shot up. "Steve Flint's wife?"

Jake nodded while he spread cream cheese on his bagel.

"Why?" Jolene felt her heart tug. Steve Flint had grown up in Noquitt and had been a close friend of her sister, Celeste. He'd been over to the house many times and Jolene knew him well. He was a good guy. Jolene remembered when he and Gail had met—the two of them had been head over heels for each other and gotten married within six months. Surely, they weren't having trouble already? Steve had been so in love with her it was almost sickening.

"He thinks she has something going with a professor at the junior college and she meets him around ten. I guess he doesn't have classes then." Jake gestured to the top of her desk. "I put some pictures of her in that folder for you."

"Okay," Jolene glanced at the clock. Plenty of time to get to the college by ten. She flipped open the folder. Inside were a few shots of the beautiful blonde. "I already know what she looks like. Steve is a friend of the family."

"Oh? I hope she won't recognize you tailing her."

Jolene shrugged. "We don't know each other that well, but if she spots me I'll just pretend we've run into each other by coincidence. It's understandable in a small town like this."

"We also need to figure out how to get evidence for the Powers case."

"Oh, right," Jolene licked some cream cheese off the side of her bagel. "The feud."

Jake laughed. "I know it seems silly, but Jeb was pretty mad about those lobster pots. It's his livelihood."

"Oh, I know. You never screw with a lobsterman's traps." Jolene scrunched up the empty bagel bag and tossed it into the trash barrel beside her desk. "But do you really think Gordy did something to them? I mean, I know they've had that feud going on for a while, but messing with someone's traps is hitting below the belt."

Jake pursed his lips together. "I thought that, too, but Jeb is pretty sure *something* happened, so I guess we'd better dig into it."

"Okay, I'll check out the satellite pictures later on. Maybe one of them caught someone messing around with the lobster traps."

"Maybe you can go down to the cove and check out the boats to see if you can see anything. I doubt Gordy will let you on his, but you can see a lot from the dock." Jake glanced out the window at the ocean. "In the meantime, I'll hit the streets and ask around. You know how quickly rumors spread through the fishermen grapevine around here."

Jolene nodded. The fishermen were worse than the blue-haired old ladies under the hair-dryers down at Mavis' *Cut-N-Curl* when it came to gossip.

"Oh, and Luke called," Jake continued, "sounded like he might have something for us, too."

Jolene cocked an eyebrow at Jake. "Oh? Another mysterious assignment?"

Luke Hunter was Morgan's high school sweetheart who had left her to join the military, then suddenly appeared in town again two summers ago. He now worked for some secret agency that he refused to give them details about.

The odd thing was that the agency seemed to know all about Jolene and her sisters and their special 'gifts' and was keen to hire them to help out on cases. They'd already completed one assignment that involved digging up an old treasure out West and it had proven to be interesting work. Jolene still had no idea what this had to do with the government—or even *if* it did—but she wasn't about to look a gift horse in the mouth.

Jake shrugged. "He didn't say exactly, just that he'd heard rumblings about something being up."

"Well, I can't wait to see what that's all about." Jolene slid out from behind the desk and made her way to the door, stopping with her hand on the knob. "Are you gonna be over for supper tonight? My long lost aunt is coming to visit."

Jake looked up from his laptop screen, his lips cocked in a crooked smile. "I heard. Wouldn't miss meeting another Blackmoore woman for anything. The rest of you have all been so fascinating."

Jolene pulled the door open, shoved her oversized sunglasses on her face and looked back at Jake over the top of them.

"You can say that again," she said, then disappeared out into the hall.

Chapter Three

"Do you remember much about Aunt Eliza?" Morgan looked across the cottage at Fiona who was bent over a gold and amethyst necklace laid out on her worktable.

Fiona glanced up, her ice-blue eyes narrowing slightly. "Gosh, we were just kids when she went away. I don't remember much about her."

Morgan pressed her lips together. She didn't remember much about Eliza either—she'd been too preoccupied with teenage things to pay much attention to an adult aunt, even if Eliza was only ten years older than she was.

She turned toward the tall, rustic shelf that housed her selection of dried herbs in old-fashioned glass apothecary jars. She loved the look of the jars, which she'd acquired at yard sales and auctions, all lined up on the wooden shelves that were accented with layers of chipped paint.

The cottage that housed *Sticks and Stones* had been in the family for generations and sat on a large parcel of land about two miles from their home. Their ancestor, Isaiah Blackmoore, a sailing merchant, had settled the town. Rumor had it that he originally owned all the land from their house on the point to the cottage, but most of it had been sold off over the generations.

For some reason, the family had always kept this cottage and Morgan was glad. The one story cottage was small, but she loved it here.

They hadn't done much to it in order to convert it into a store. It was already one big room. They split the main room with Morgan and her herbs on the left and Fiona and her crystals on the right. Behind the main room were a small bedroom and a bathroom. What had once been the kitchen area was on Morgan's side and she'd removed cabinets and appliances, then rearranged it a bit to fit in her herb displays. The sink came in handy for making her remedies, which, she realized, she should be doing now.

She glanced out the window over the sink. The rose bushes that matched the ones growing along the front porch were starting to bloom. Birds chirped and twittered as they flitted between the branches of the trees in the woods behind the cottage. If she squinted and looked directly to the back of the woods, she could make out a faint line of sparkling blue ocean a half-mile away.

She turned her attention back to the shelves, the old pine floorboards sighing as she reached up to pull down the jars of lemon verbena and oregano. Laying out some mesh tea bags, she took a pinch out of each jar and placed them in the middle of the bags, touching the herbs gently with her fingertips so as to infuse them with as much healing energy as possible.

"Do you think Eliza has any unusual, umm ... gifts ... you know, like us?" Morgan asked.

Fiona squinted down at the necklace. The amethyst stone glowed slightly when her fingers brushed against it. She answered without looking up. "I hadn't thought about it. You'd think we would have heard if she did. I never heard of anyone else in the family having them."

"Me either, but just because we haven't heard about it doesn't mean no one else has them."

"Still, I don't think we should let on that *we* do. I mean, we all agreed the less people that know the better."

"Yep, that's true." The girls had discovered early on that it wasn't a good idea to let too many people know about their paranormal powers. People tended to react strangely and it was better to keep that kind of thing to themselves.

"I wonder if she'll want to poke around in the attic," Fiona said.

Morgan began the process of folding the mesh tea bags over the herbs to secure them. "That's a good question. That stuff is hers as much as it is ours. Some of it may even have more sentimental value for her, especially if she remembers it from her childhood."

Fiona glanced up. "We haven't even seen everything up there ourselves."

"I know. There might be other important historical items like that journal," Morgan said, referring to an old book they'd discovered in the attic. The book had been written three hundred years earlier by Isaiah Blackmoore and contained coded clues about a mysterious family legacy. The girls had discovered the meaning of the journal along with an attic full of treasure already, but the attic was so large they hadn't explored the whole thing. Morgan had a gut feeling there could be more family mysteries up in the attic, and her gut feelings were usually right.

"... and the crystals," Fiona added, referring to a mysterious burlap sack they'd found with crystals inside like the ones Fiona used in her healing jewelry. Apparently, a long-ago ancestor had the same affinity for stones. But had they also possessed Fiona's healing powers?

"Well, if she needs money, we have plenty now. We should be sharing it with her anyway, since it came from her ancestors, too. Just because Dad inherited the house doesn't mean he should have everything in it, too."

"I agree." Fiona said. "They probably didn't even realize anything of value was up in the attic. Everyone thought it was just cast-offs and junk. It's an awkward subject, though. It's not like we can just come out and ask her if she needs money."

"Right. I guess we'll just play it by ear."

The girls were interrupted by the cheerful tinkle of the bells on front door. That sound always made Morgan feel happy—it signaled the arrival of a paying customer.

Two little old ladies came through the door, their heavy orthopedic shoes clomping on the wooden flooring.

"Morning Beatrice." Morgan nodded at the woman on the left, then nodded to the one on the right. "Harriet."

"Morning girls," the two women chorused.

"I've come for my herbal teas." Beatrice marched over to the counter that separated Morgan's half of the shop from the main area.

"I'm just finishing them up now," Morgan said as she tied the last teabag and then placed all the tea bags into a white paper shopping bag that sat on the counter.

Harriet eyed the two apothecary jars.

"Lemon Verbena and Oregano." She pursed her wrinkly lips and looked at Beatrice. "Now why would you need a tea made from those herbs?"

"Never you mind," Beatrice shot back.

Morgan rang up the sale, ignoring the two women's banter. She wasn't about to betray a customer's confidence and tell Harriet that the remedy was for flatulence.

"We heard your Aunt Eliza is coming back to town," Beatrice said as she fished in her large handbag for her wallet.

Morgan raised a brow at Fiona. News sure did travel fast in this town. "Yep, we're excited to see her. None of us remember much about her."

"Your grandma was right put out when Eliza up and left like that," Harriet said while they all watched Beatrice take her time counting out the exact change.

"Just why *did* she leave?" Morgan frowned at Harriet.

Harriet and Beatrice glanced sideways at each other. "Oh, we really couldn't say..."

"Surely it can't be a secret after all this time?" Morgan prompted.

Beatrice pushed the pile of change and bills toward Morgan. "No, we really couldn't say because we don't know why."

"We always figured she just didn't want to be tied down in a small town," Harried added.

"I guess that makes sense." Morgan rang up the change.

"Well, we must be going." Beatrice grabbed her bag and turned toward the door.

"Ta-ta," Harried said, following Beatrice.

As the two women exited the shop, Morgan mulled over what they had said about Eliza leaving town. It made sense that Eliza left because she had dreams that couldn't be satisfied in a small town. What didn't make sense was that she left and never talked to anyone in the family ever again—until now.

Chapter Four

Jolene slouched down in the seat of her car and stared at the concrete exterior of the junior college. The picture of Gail Flint sat beside her on the passenger seat. She didn't really need the picture, though. She knew Gail personally and besides, every detail of the woman was imprinted in her photographic memory.

At nine-fifty-five, a green Subaru pulled up. Jolene watched Gail Flint get out and walk into the building.

That's strange, she thought. Normally, cheating spouses had clandestine evening rendezvous at some out of the way place to conduct their affair, but here was Gail trotting right into the school in broad daylight.

Jolene chewed on her bottom lip, deciding whether to follow her or wait out here. As she stared at the building, trying to make up her mind, she felt the hairs on the back of her neck prickle ... as if someone was watching her.

Her back stiffened, but she kept her head facing forward as she glanced up at the rear-view mirror, then slid her eyes to the side mirrors. She didn't see anyone there. Slowly she reached up to the rear-view mirror, angling it to see more of the parking lot behind her.

A spark of sunlight glinted off something at the very back of the lot near the woods. Jolene spun around in her seat.

Was someone back there with binoculars or a camera?

Why would someone be watching her? Before she could even think of the answer, she found herself ripping the door open and bolting out of the car.

She sprinted toward the woods. The glint disappeared. The bushes rustled where she thought she'd seen someone, then they fell back in place. When she got to the spot, no one was there.

"Damn it!"

She stared into the woods, but the only thing that moved was a squirrel scurrying down the trunk of an old oak tree. She turned her attention to the area where she thought she'd seen someone. The brush was trampled, branches broken.

Someone *had* been there.

But had they been watching her? And, if so, why?

Jolene was just coming out of the woods onto the paved surface of the parking lot when she saw Gail Flint come out of the building. She held back —she'd stick out like a sore thumb being the only other person in the parking lot and she didn't want Gail to see her now because it might raise suspicions if she happened to see Jolene tailing her later on.

She watched as the blonde got in her car and drove away. Alone.

Jolene looked at her watch. Gail had been in the building less than ten minutes. That certainly wasn't long enough for any nefarious activity ... not that she thought the couple would be having their affair right in the college. But it seemed odd that Gail would come here to see him. In her experience, most people having affairs tried not to be seen together in public.

Feeling a bit down that she hadn't made any headway on the case, Jolene decided to proceed to the next task on her list—questioning the only witness that saw her mother jump to her death.

***

Earl Whiting lived in a ramshackle old house on the outskirts of Noquitt. Jolene pulled into the dirt driveway at eleven-thirty—a time when most lobstermen were out pulling their traps. She figured Earl would be home, though, since he wasn't known to keep regular hours.

Jolene had known Earl her whole life and the entire town knew he worked as little as possible, preferring to spend his days with a six-pack.

Jolene parked in the middle of the yard—if you could even call it a yard. It was more like a dump with piles of junk here and there and not a blade of grass in sight. The main house was a small white cottage. Its screen door hung half open, squeaking loudly as the breeze moved it back and forth.

To the left of the main house was a chicken coop, the chickens long gone. To the left of the coop, a barn leaned dangerously, the roof sporting bare patches where shingles, now resting in the yard, had blown off.

Her shoes crunched over the glass from a broken bottle as she approached the house. The sounds of a television game show blared from an open window next to the door where a soiled curtain fluttered in the breeze.

Jolene knocked on the door and waited a few seconds, then knocked louder.

"Yeah, I'm comin'," She heard Earl yell just before he ripped the door open.

Jolene took a step backward and looked up at the red-faced man in front of her. Despite his skinny arms and legs, his stomach strained at the dirty white t-shirt he wore. His gray hair stuck up from the top of his head in an unruly mess.

He squinted down at her. "Wadda ya want?"

"Hi, Earl, It's me, Jolene Blackmoore."

He leaned closer and the smell of stale beer and cigarettes hit her like a tidal wave, causing her to take a step back.

His eyes widened. "Oh, so it is. Didn't recognize ya' ... It's been a few years and you done growed up."

His eyes drifted down to Jolene's chest and she bit the inside of her cheek to stop herself from giving him a piece of her mind.

"What brings ya' here?" He looked back up at her eyes.

Jolene peered up at him from under her lashes. She figured playing the helpless, cute female would get more answers out of him than being tough and demanding.

She softened her voice. "Well, I know you set your lobster pots just outside the point near my house..."

"Yeah..." Earl's eyes narrowed.

"I was wondering ... well," Jolene looked down at her feet, trying to appear vulnerable and appeal to his sense of wanting to help. "I wondered if you saw anything the day my mother died."

She looked up at him, plastering a look of wide-eyed innocence on her face. She didn't want to give on that she was actually investigating and had seen the police report. She'd get more answers from him if she pretended she was just a girl interested in finding out about her momma's death.

"What do you mean?" His white eyebrows mashed together.

Jolene's eyes drifted over his shoulder into the house. The big screen TV—one of the older, bulky models—and leather theater seating seemed at odds in the tiny, old-fashioned living room.

"Well, they say she jumped, but I have a hard time believing that. I mean, I knew my mother. She was happy."

"I don't know anything that can help you." Earl turned away and started to shut the door.

"Wait!" Her plea caused him to turn back toward her. "But you did see her that day, right?"

Jolene focused on his aura. Normally she filtered the aura energy out—it was too distracting for normal interaction, but now she wanted to get a bead on Earl's state of mind. As she suspected, his aura was white with bands of red, gray and brown. Earl was ill—probably with alcoholism or maybe even something more serious. His aura also showed he was oriented toward materialistic things, and, more importantly, the brown and gray showed that he had unsettling thoughts and possibly bad intentions.

Earl's hands fidgeted on the door, his eyes darted left and right. He didn't look Jolene in the eye as he said, "I saw her, and like I told the police, she was alone on the cliff."

Then he slammed the door shut in her face.

Jolene stood facing the door for a few seconds. Earl hadn't told her much, but the way he acted and his aura had told her plenty.

Earl Whiting had something to hide.

As she turned to go back to her car, she noticed the barn and its half-open door. She couldn't resist taking a peek inside. Glancing back at the house to make sure Earl wasn't watching her, she walked over and stood just outside the barn door. Shading her eyes against the sun, she squinted into the dark interior.

On the right was a shiny speedboat on a trailer. She knew Earl moored his old, run-down lobster boat at Perkins Cove, but she never knew he had a speedboat.

Next to the boat was a Suburban. It looked to be in good condition—not this year's model, though—probably a few years old.

Jolene chewed her bottom lip as she stared at the car and boat. From what she knew about Earl, he didn't have enough money for these expensive items, not to mention the big television and theatre seating in his house. Even though the items seemed to be years old, and he could have bought them used, things still didn't add up.

"I heard you talkin' ta Earl," a soft voice said in Jolene's ear. She whirled around to see Earl's wife, Mae, standing at the corner of the barn. A worn white t-shirt hung from her tiny frame. The bottom of the shirt came almost down to her knees, but didn't quite cover the holes in her faded jeans. She held a planter with freshly planted purple pansies in her lime-green, gardening-gloved hands.

"Hi, Mae. You startled me," Jolene said.

"Sorry, child." Mae's eyes slid over to the house. Her face was deeply etched with the lines of hard work and harsh Maine winters. Jolene knew she was probably only in her late fifties, but she looked twenty years older. She guessed being married to Earl had probably sped up the aging process.

"I heard what Earl told ya' about yer ma."

"Yes," Jolene prompted.

"I always liked Johanna." Mae's eyes clouded. "She was always nice to me even when others weren't."

"I remember that about her." Jolene's heart warmed, remembering how her mother was always kind to anyone, no matter what their circumstances or how the townspeople felt about them.

"Anyway," Mae leaned closer to Jolene and lowered her voice. "What Earl said ... I don't know if it's the whole truth."

Jolene's brows shot up. "Really? What *is* the truth?"

"Well, I'm not sure 'bout that." Mae's voice was barely above a whisper now, her eyes darting nervously back to the house. "But I might know where you can find out."

The front door to the house opened and Mae's face took on a look of terror.

"Mae? What 'cha telling that girl?" Earl bellowed from the doorway.

"Nuttin', Earl, just trading planting tips for the season," Mae said, backing away from Jolene.

Jolene's heart plummeted. She grabbed Mae's elbow.

"Wait," she whispered, hoping Earl couldn't hear her. "How can I find out the truth?"

Mae glanced wide-eyed at the house, then turned back to Jolene and mouthed the words, "Andrea June."

Jolene released Mae's elbow and Mae scurried toward the house, setting the potted plant down on the steps as she scooted past Earl and into the living room.

Earl glared at Jolene from the doorway.

"You best be goin' now." He jerked his chin toward Jolene's car.

"Right. See ya." Jolene hopped into her car, turned the engine over and drove off without even a glance in the rear-view mirror.

As she pulled out onto the road, she felt a ray of hope—she'd been given a clue that might help her find out the truth about her mother's death.

There was just one problem with the clue. She had no idea who the heck Andrea June was or where she could find her.

Chapter Five

By the time Jolene got back to the office, the village was abuzz with activity and she had to park in the public parking lot one street over. As she made her way down the street, the familiar prickle at the back of her neck caused her stomach to tighten. She slowed her pace, then stopped in front of a boutique, pretending to admire the bright yellow bathing suit in the window.

Tourists crowded the brick-paved sidewalk, sauntering along with shopping bags in their hands. Jolene scanned the crowd through the reflection in the window, her heart skipping when she saw a familiar silhouette a few stores down. The man stood still in the bustling crowd, watching her.

She whipped around, facing the man, but he wasn't there! Her eyes darted quickly to the left, then the right just in time to see the familiar crop of brown curly hair disappear down a side street.

"Hey, wait!" she called out, then ran toward the side street, jostling shoppers and causing a little boy to drop his ice cream. Ignoring the irate cries of the mother, she turned the corner, only to find an empty street.

"What the ...?" Jolene spun around looking in every direction but the man had disappeared.

She turned and headed back toward the office, her face etched with lines of confusion.

She must have been mistaken when she'd seen the silhouette, because the man she'd thought she'd seen was a friend. Even though he was somewhat mysterious and appeared at the oddest times, she couldn't imagine why he would run away from her. He'd always helped her in the past. Why would he spy on her and run away now?

She was still pondering this as she climbed the steps to her office. The sound of men's voices drifted through the closed door as she approached.

She tentatively opened the door and looked down into the hopeful face of Steve Flint. He sat in Jake's guest chair, his red-rimmed eyes searching her face.

"Hi, Steve." Jolene glanced from Steve to Jake. She knew Steve had probably come to ask if they'd found anything out about Gail and she felt bad that she wouldn't have anything concrete to tell him.

"Did you find out anything?" Steve twisted in his chair to face her.

"I'm afraid not." Jolene's heart pinched at the crestfallen look on his face. "I saw her at the school, but she wasn't doing anything suspicious."

"But you saw her meet him?"

"Not specifically. I didn't want to make her suspicious by following her inside. She was only inside for a few minutes, though. She could have gone in for anything."

"And then where did she go?"

Jolene chewed on her bottom lip. She was afraid he was going to ask that. "I didn't follow her."

"Oh ... why?"

Jolene looked from Steve to Jake again. She didn't want to tell them it was because she was halfway across the parking lot chasing someone she thought was watching her. "I just felt it was better not to. It would be too obvious and, since Gail knows me, I was afraid it might make following her in the future problematic if she saw me today."

That seemed to satisfy them and it was mostly true. She probably wouldn't have followed Gail anyway because she was alone. Better to wait until she felt there would be a compromising moment to witness.

Steve deflated. "I just want it to be over with. I knew I never should have married someone so beautiful ... but I still love her."

Jolene leaned her hip on the corner of Jake's desk and looked down at Steve. "What makes you so sure she's having an affair?"

"Well, look at me." Steve spread his hands. "What would someone like *her* want with someone like *me*?"

Jolene tilted her head. Steve didn't look so bad and she knew he was a nice guy. "Don't be so hard on yourself. You're a nice guy."

"Well, you know what they say about nice guys." Steve rubbed his hands across his face. "Anyway, she's been sneaking off and acting secretive. I know she's hiding something and it's got to be an affair."

"What makes you think it's with someone at the college?"

"I heard her talking on the phone to a friend. She mentioned something about the college but when she realized I was listening she got all nervous and tried to cover it up." Steve sighed. "It all adds up. I knew she was too pretty for me. The sad thing is I still love her ... even if she doesn't clean the house and can't cook worth a damn."

Jake stood and Steve took the hint, pushing himself up from the chair.

"We'll do our best to find out exactly what's going on as soon as possible." Jake clapped his hand on Steve's shoulder and gave Jolene a pointed look.

Jolene slid behind her desk, just as Jake was escorting Steve out the door. "Hey, do either of you know someone named Andrea June?" she asked.

Steve's brow creased. "No. Why? Does it have something to do with Gail?"

"No ... it's just someone I need to talk to."

Jake shook his head. "Nope. Sorry. Don't know any June's at all. Is that the last name?"

Jolene pursed her lips. She hadn't considered that June might be the middle name. If that were the case, not having her last name would make the search much more difficult. "Good question. I'm not sure."

"So, you'll let me know as soon as you find anything?" Steve pleaded.

"Of course," Jake said.

Steve disappeared down the hall and Jake turned to Jolene. "So, you really didn't find anything out about Gail's affair?"

"No. She went in and came out. Not enough time for any funny business, though. I didn't follow her because I felt like someone was following *me*," she confessed.

Jake's brows knit together. "Why would someone follow you?"

"I have no idea. It's weird, but I thought I saw someone watching me out on the street, too." Jolene glanced out the window to the street below but didn't see the familiar figure. "Anyway, I'm not so sure about Gail. If she was having an affair with a professor, I doubt she'd go in and visit him like that in the middle of the day."

"Yeah, usually people having affairs don't meet at each other's workplaces. Maybe she had to give him an urgent message and couldn't call for some reason?"

"Maybe."

Jake leaned across his desk and grabbed his keys. "I'm going to ask around town about the Powers-Ellis feud."

"Okay, I'll get on the computer and see if I can dig up any satellite photos that give us some clues about that case." Jolene flipped open her laptop and pressed the space bar to bring her computer to life.

"See you tonight." Jake closed the door, leaving Jolene alone to focus on the computer. But not the satellite photos. She went straight to the town residents database in search of Andrea June.

Three hours and several databases later, she still hadn't found her. She'd searched births, deaths and licenses to no avail.

Jolene closed the computer with a sigh, stood up and stretched out the kinks in her back. It was time to go home and re-meet her estranged aunt.

Chater Six

Jolene lifted the lid on the cast iron pot, inhaling deeply until her nose was filled with the sweet aroma of cream and clams. Clam chowder was her favorite and no one made it like her sister, Fiona.

"Hey, no tasting!" Fiona appeared at the kitchen door in a lavender silk sleeveless blouse and faded blue jeans. "It needs to simmer a little more for all the flavors to meld together."

Jolene dropped the lid back onto the pot. "It's like torture. You know that's my favorite."

"You'll get plenty once Eliza gets here and we sit down to eat," Morgan chimed in from the pantry where she was standing on her tiptoes pulling the 'good' glassware from the top shelf.

Morgan's white linen top hugged her slim curves and made her dark hair look even blacker. Jolene looked down at her own outfit of black t-shirt and capris self-consciously.

"Am I under-dressed?"

Morgan peeked her head back in. "Nope, not at all. We don't have to dress up. It's just an informal dinner."

"I didn't dress up, either." Celeste padded in from the hallway dressed in her usual outfit—light blue yoga pants and a swirly loose purple and blue print top.

Morgan took the crystal wine glasses to the sink to rinse them out. "Eliza should be here any minute. Is anyone else nervous?"

The four sisters looked at each other. Truth was, Jolene did feel a little nervous and she could tell her sisters did, too.

"Let's wait in the foyer so we can greet her as soon as she gets here." Fiona started down the hallway to the front door.

The foyer was a large, open space where the front door, openings to the dining room and formal living room, and stairs converged. It wasn't fancy like in some large homes, but it was nice with polished oak flooring and a carved oak staircase and moldings.

The front door gaped open. Jolene could see out past the front porch to the circular driveway. Beyond that, the view included the quaint shops and boats of Perkins Cove. She walked up to the screen door where the scent of fried clams from the restaurants in the cove mixed with the sting of the ocean air, creating a contrast to the sweet smell of Fiona's clam chowder coming from the kitchen.

The sun was low in the cloud-dotted sky. It would be setting in an hour, but the patches of sunlight dotting the driveway were still bright.

"Do you think we'll recognize her?" Fiona asked.

"She's probably changed a lot since we last saw her," Morgan answered.

"I only have fuzzy memories of her," Celeste said.

Jolene didn't remember her at all. She pursed her lips, trying to conjure up an image of Aunt Eliza. To her left, a small sailboat drifted by on the wide channel of water that led to the cove where the locals moored their fishing boats. To her right, beams of sunlight danced off the waves of the Atlantic Ocean just beyond the cliff. Which reminded her of her mother.

"Do any of you know someone named Andrea June?"

Morgan's forehead creased. "I don't think so."

Fiona shook her head.

"Not that I can remember," Celeste shrugged. "Why do you ask?"

"Oh, just a case I'm on."

The sounds of tires on gravel pulled their attention away and Jolene felt grateful for the change of subject as all heads swiveled in the direction of the driveway where the Noquitt taxi was pulling to a stop.

"She's here." Fiona said softly.

Jolene watched a purple flip-flop clad foot appear from the back door of the car followed by a slim pale leg in purple capri pants and deep-purple tank top. Her Aunt Eliza's long, silver-white hair flowed past her shoulders as she tipped the cab driver and retrieved her luggage—a small purple bag on wheels.

The sun ducked behind a cloud and a shadow fell over Eliza's face as she turned her ice-blue eyes toward the house. Celeste rushed out the door and swooped her into a hug.

Eliza suffered Celeste's exuberant greeting looking a bit taken aback.

"Welcome, Aunt Eliza!" Celeste released her.

"Thanks. I know you must be Celeste, but it's been such a long time I barely recognize you," Eliza said in her soft, melodic voice, the sound of which struck a familiar chord in Jolene's heart. She must have remembered the distinctive tone from her childhood.

Morgan pushed the screen door open and the rest of them came out onto the porch as Celeste took Eliza's luggage and led her up the steps.

"Morgan?" Eliza tilted her head as she inspected the oldest Blackmoore sister.

"Auntie Eliza, we've missed you." Morgan hugged Eliza, then the two women broke apart and Eliza turned to face Fiona, reaching out to run a lock of Fiona's red curls through her fingers.

"I'd recognize these red curls anywhere," Eliza said then her eyes hardened. "My mother's hair was the same shade of red."

Eliza and Fiona hugged and then it was Jolene's turn. Eliza stepped in front of her and studied her face.

"And Jolene ... you were just a baby when I left." Jolene smiled and hugged Eliza. Her small frame felt fragile.

Eliza held her at arm's length again, then her gaze drifted to the locket on her neck and Jolene saw her eyes widen. A shadow crossed her face. For a split second, Eliza looked almost panicked, but then she composed herself, abruptly turning and looking out at the ocean.

"I see the house has been kept up nicely and the view is still superb." Eliza spread her arms to indicate the scenic view from their porch, which encompassed the channel and cove to the left and ocean to the right.

"We tried to do our best. There're still some repairs that we need to catch up on," Morgan said.

Eliza was still staring out at the ocean. Jolene saw her eyes narrow as she looked at the cliff ... or rather, the section of cliff that was missing.

"What happened over there?" Eliza pointed in the direction of her gaze.

The sisters exchanged an uneasy look. The side of the cliff had been blown away when modern day pirates came to the Blackmoore estate to hunt for treasure. Due to the unusual and somewhat paranormal circumstances, it was an event the Blackmoore sisters didn't care to talk about ... even to their aunt.

"The face of the cliff crumbled into the ocean." Fiona recited the story they'd all agreed on.

Eliza turned back to them, her eyes narrowed. "Really? How unfortunate."

The five women stared at each other and Jolene got the distinct impression that Eliza knew they were lying.

Fiona broke the uncomfortable silence "I hope you're hungry. We have a seaside feast prepared, including my famous clam chowder."

She held open the screen door then turned to Eliza. "I hope you like seafood."

"But of course." Eliza stepped into the house and stood frozen in the foyer with Morgan, Fiona, Jolene and Celeste behind her. She looked to the left and right, then up the stairs. "This hasn't changed a bit. It feels almost like I've stepped back in time."

"We've made some changes since your time here, but not in the foyer," Morgan said.

"We think the foyer is pretty much perfect the way it is," Celeste added. "But wait until you see the kitchen."

"First, though," Morgan cut in. "We wanted to ask you to stay here with us."

Eliza raised her left brow. "Oh? Well, I don't want to impose."

"No, we insist." Celeste pulled Eliza's suitcase closer, as if she would hold it for ransom should Eliza decide to go to a hotel.

Eliza shrugged. "Well, then, I guess it's decided."

"Meow!" Belladonna appeared seemingly out of nowhere and proceeded to turn figure eights around Eliza's ankles.

"Bella!" Eliza's face lit with surprise. She bent down to pet the cat who rubbed her face on Eliza's hand, purring loudly. "Wait. You can't be Bella ... Bella would be too old now."

"That's Belladonna," Jolene said. "We've had her for ages. I remember we always had a white cat, but I'm not sure how old Belladonna is."

"We always had a white cat, too." Eliza frowned up at the girls.

"Maybe they're related," Morgan said. "She could be one of Bella's kittens."

"Or even one of her kittens' kittens."

Jolene looked down at the cat who slowly lowered her eyes to contented slits. They'd had Belladonna ever since she could remember—how old *was* she?

"So. It's settled, then. Celeste started toward the stairs, tugging Eliza's suitcase after her. "I'm sure you know this place as good as we do. Which room do you want?"

Eliza stood, her gaze drifting up the stairs. "I guess I'll take my old room if no one else is using it."

"Which one is that?"

"West wing, on the end."

The girls exchanged a look. They'd always felt the west wing was rather dark and foreboding. They never went there. And the room on the end was decorated in vintage gothic style, complete with an intricately dark carved wood mantle and red velvet wallpaper on one wall. It was the furthest room from the main household activity, but if that's what their guest wanted, that's what they'd give her.

"It's empty, but I'll need do a little freshening up and put new sheets on the bed," Morgan said. "You guys give Eliza a tour of the downstairs while I do that and then it should be time to eat."

"I guess we can start with familiar territory," Fiona said as Morgan took the luggage from

Celeste and headed upstairs. "I don't think the living room has changed much since you lived here."

Celeste was closest to the living room entrance, so she led the way inside the large room. The front of the room boasted long, wide windows framed with green velveteen drapes. The edges of the wide pine floor peeked out from under a green and gold oriental rug. The room was dotted with antique furniture from various Blackmoore generations.

"It does look much the same." Eliza's eyes scanned the room. She pointed to the overstuffed green brocade sofa and matching chair. "New sofa though. My mother always kept that stuffy Victorian set in here."

"That's up in the attic now," Jolene said.

"There's a lot of stuff up there." Eliza glanced up at the ceiling and Jolene thought she saw a strange expression flicker across her face just before Fiona captured their attention by sliding the wood-paneled pocket doors open, revealing the library.

"My favorite room," Eliza said turning toward the room with its giant bookcase walls. The tufted leather sofa and chairs sat stoically as they had for decades and Jolene wasn't surprised when Eliza recognized them.

"Grandpa's furniture," Celeste ran her hand lovingly along the back of the sofa. "This is my favorite room, too. It's so quiet and peaceful."

Eliza nodded in agreement, studying the room almost as if she was looking for something.

"It's quiet because the books absorb sound." Jolene crossed the jewel-toned oriental carpet and opened the door at the other end of the room leading them out into the hall.

Across the hall was the east parlor and its expansive view of the Atlantic Ocean. They led Eliza in there and she looked around the room in wonder.

"Boy, has this room changed," she said.

"Yeah, our mom redecorated it shortly before she ... died," Celeste said.

Jolene could see a sad, faraway look reflected in Eliza's eyes as she glanced out at the cliff ... at the very spot form which Johanna had jumped.

Eliza turned back toward the room, her eyes cast down at her feet. "I'm really sorry about your mom. She was like a big sister to me. I wanted to come back when it happened ... but I couldn't."

Jolene's heart tugged for the other woman.

What had happened that was so terrible it kept Eliza from returning for her sister-in-law's funeral?

No one knew what to say. The awkward silence stretched on, punctuated by the ticking of the grandmother clock in the hall until Morgan appeared in the doorway to the kitchen.

"Okay, your room is all set up and I think dinner is ready," she said. "You guys want to eat?"

"Absolutely." Celeste started toward the door.

"My chowder!" Fiona bolted for the kitchen.

Morgan turned back into the kitchen and Eliza started toward her slowly with Jolene lagging behind at the edge of the room.

As she left, Eliza cast one long glance out the window toward the ocean. Jolene concentrated her senses to read the other woman's aura.

Her aura showed bands of purple to match Eliza's outfit. Jolene wondered if Eliza had paranormal gifts too. Purple indicated spiritual thoughts—she might have gifts and she might not even know, or maybe she was religious. But there was another color in her aura that set Jolene's nerves on edge—gray.

Jolene felt a prickle of unease in her stomach as she watched her aunt disappear through the door into the kitchen. She had no idea why Eliza had suddenly shown up after all these years, but one thing she did know was that her long lost aunt had a secret.

Chapter Seven

Jolene sat on the edge of her bed, her feet flat on the hard wooden floor, trying to wake herself up. Jake, Luke and Celeste's boyfriend, and long-time Blackmoore family friend, Cal, had arrived just in time for dinner and had stayed up well into the night filling Eliza in on town gossip.

Luke and Cal were both townies and Eliza remembered their families and even embarrassed Cal by telling a funny story of when he was a young boy. Of course, she didn't know Jake since he was new in town. Thoughts of Jake reminded Jolene that she'd better get a move-on. She was supposed to go down to Perkins Cove to dig up information about 'the feud' and she wanted to get an early start. She hadn't been very productive on either one of her cases and wanted to put in a full day so she could make some progress before Jake got on her case.

But first ... coffee.

She threw on jeans, a t-shirt and sneakers, then swirled her chocolate brown hair into a high pony tail before heading down to the kitchen.

Celeste was already up and at the counter making her wheat grass concoction. Jolene headed straight for the k-cup machine to make herself a cup of strong, dark roast.

"Morning!" Celeste's perpetually cheerful chirp grated on Jolene. She couldn't take 'cheerful' until she'd had at least half a cup of caffeine.

"Hi." Jolene settled into one of the stools at the kitchen island.

"Did you sleep well?" Celeste asked.

"Like a baby. You?"

Celeste nodded. "I wonder if Eliza is an early riser."

Jolene shrugged, preferring to focus on drinking her coffee instead of talking.

"What are you up to today?" Celeste asked after a few minutes of silence.

"This morning I'm heading down to Perkins Cove to ask around about Gordy fooling with Jed's traps. Then this afternoon I have a lot of computer work to do."

"I could walk down to the cove with you if you want. I have to drop some lavender oil Morgan made off to my friend, Darlene, at *A Scent of Maine*," Celeste said, referring to one of the boutique shops in the cove that sold perfumes and oils.

Perkins Cove was comprised of a small, horseshoe shaped piece of land that abutted the Blackmoore land. On one side was the cove that housed a variety of fishing, pleasure and sightseeing boats. The land next to it was filled with three rows of old fishermen's shacks made into quaint boutique stores and restaurants. Back in the day, only fishermen came here, but somewhere along the line someone realized how picturesque the small cove with its wooden, manually-operated drawbridge was and it didn't take long for it to become a popular tourist destination. Soon, the old shacks had been turned into stores and restaurants.

"Okay. Sure." Truth was, Jolene could use the company. She'd been considering confiding in Celeste about her search for the truth about their mother. She could use someone to bounce ideas off of and she was closest to Celeste. She would be less resistant to the idea of trying to find out what really happened than their older sisters.

Celeste cleaned up the juicer while Jolene waited for the caffeine to hit her brain. After a few minutes, she put her mug in the sink.

"You ready, or do you need to change?"

Celeste looked down at her black yoga pants and white t-shirt. "No. I'm ready. Let's go."

Stepping off the front porch, they both took a deep breath of salty sea air. 'I never get tired of that smell," Celeste said.

"Me, either. I love it first thing in the morning before the restaurants start up and the smell of fried seafood gets into the air."

The Blackmoore house was set at the very point of land where the channel to the cove kissed the Atlantic Ocean. Although it was on over an acre of land, it was still situated within smelling distance of the cove restaurants. It was only a mere quarter of a mile walk to the heart of the cove, which gave them the best of both worlds —the privacy and ocean view along with the convenience of close shops and restaurants. The only drawback was that sometimes they could smell those restaurants from their front porch, especially when the breeze was blowing to the south.

The walked down the driveway side by side, the gulls crying above them. Jolene was quiet, trying to think up a way to broach the subject of their mother's death.

"So, what's with this Andrea June you were asking about yesterday?" Celeste asked as if she had read her mind.

Jolene's hand flew up to the locket around her neck. "I think she might know something about Mom's death."

Celeste stopped short. "What do you mean? Mom jumped off the cliff."

"I know, but don't you think the investigation was lacking? Overton tied it up pretty quickly and there was hardly any evidence. Besides, I don't remember Mom being depressed enough to kill herself, do you?" Jolene's fingers fiddled nervously with the locket. She hoped Celeste would think about what she had to say and not just dismiss her out of hand.

Celeste's eyes darted to the locket. "Isn't that the locket that looks just like the one Mom wore?"

"Yes." Jolene pulled it away from her neck and angled her head to look at it.

"What's in it?"

"Nothing." Jolene flipped it open to show her. "Why?"

Celeste shrugged. "Oh nothing ... Grandma said something to me about the key being in the locket, but sometimes she says things that don't make much sense."

Jolene pressed her lips together and looked at the locket a few seconds before snapping it shut again. The locket had been empty when she'd found it. She had no idea what this key was or if it had anything to do with her mother's death. "So, anyway, don't you think there might be more to Mom's death than we were told?"

Celeste screwed her face up. "Well, honestly I never really thought about it. I was only a teenager at the time and I guess I just assumed the adults knew better."

"I was pretty young, too, but I remember some things didn't add up. Every time I asked a question, though, I was told to shush up. I guess that's why Overton ended up hating us so much. Maybe my nosy questions got him in trouble with his superiors."

"Well, they did find her scarf washed up on the rocks and there was a witness that saw her jump," Celeste offered.

Jolene snorted. "Earl Whiting? You know as well as I do that he's about as reliable as cable TV in a thunderstorm. Besides, I think he's hiding something." Jolene told her about Earl's expensive purchases and Mae's warning about finding the truth from Andrea June.

Celeste started walking slowly toward the cove and Jolene followed. "But surely you aren't suggesting she didn't jump."

"No, I'm just saying the circumstance might have been different than what we were led to believe." Jolene's fingers fiddled with the locket around her neck. "We owe it to her to find out for sure."

"Okay. What can I do to help?"

"For starters, don't tell Morgan or Fiona. They'll just try to get me to stop and I really feel like I'm on to something. Other than that, it will just be nice to have someone to bounce ideas off of."

"Well, you can count on me," Celeste said as they reached the main part of the cove.

"Oh, there's Josiah Littlefield." Jolene nodded toward a wiry white-haired man struggling with a lobster trap on the dock. "I want to ask him about Jeb's traps."

Josiah looked up at them as they approached. "Hi, girls. Nice day, ay?"

"It sure is," Jolene said. "I was wondering if I could ask you something."

"Ayuh." Josiah looked back down at lobster trap he was repairing, the sinewy muscles on his lean arms rippling under his leathery, tanned skin.

Not bad for an old guy, Jolene thought as she tried to figure out the best way to phrase the question.

"Have you heard anything about an issue between Gordy Ellis and Jebediah Powers?"

Josiah chuckled. "When hasn't there been an issue between those two? Those boys been goin' at it since grade school."

"I remember some of those fights," Celeste said.

"Thing is, their daddies started the feud and the boys are just carryin' it on," Josiah said.

"Jeb seems to think Gordy might have messed with his traps—says some of them are missing."

Josiah stopped what he was doing and looked at Jolene, squinting into the sun that was behind her. "Is that so? Well, I don't rightly know 'bout that, but I don' think Gordy would do that. Boy knows better than to mess with another fisherman's traps, no matter how much of a feud they got goin' on."

Jolene nodded. She felt the same way. The traps were a fisherman's livelihood and it was a low blow to mess with them.

"Got any idea who might have messed with them and why?" Jolene asked. Someone *had* messed with them—maybe it wasn't Gordy, though.

Josiah shook his head. "Sorry, don't know nuttin' 'bout that."

"Okay, thanks." Jolene turned to go, took a step, then turned back. "Hey, Josiah, you don't know where I could find Andrea June, do you?"

To her surprise, Josiah nodded.

"Ayuh. I reckon she be right over there." He pointed to a stack of boats moored at the edge of the cove.

Jolene's heart soared with hope. "She has a boat?"

"Nope," Josiah said.

Jolene scrunched up her face at him. "But you pointed at the boats."

Celeste cut in before Josiah could answer. "Not *has* a boat ... *is* a boat."

Jolene squinted in the direction Celeste was looking. Four boats were moored right next to each other. The furthest was a dilapidated old lobster boat that looked like it might sink on the spot. As the boats moved in the shallow waves, that boat edged forward far enough for Jolene to read the name on the front.

Andrea June.

Chapter Eight

Celeste was starting to regret making the trip to the cove with Jolene.

Too late now, she thought as she sat crammed into the dinghy Jolene had commandeered from an old high school friend she'd run into on the dock.

A sense of foreboding came over her as the *Andrea June* loomed closer and closer. White paint chips dotted her side, giving away the original color of the now dull-gray boat. Clusters of barnacles stuck out from the boat at the water line. It had been a long time since anyone had cared for the *Andrea June*. Josiah had said he hadn't seen the boat leave the cove in years, but someone had to be paying the mooring bill, otherwise it wouldn't still be here.

Jolene pulled the dinghy alongside the boat and tied it off to the mooring where the rope from the *Andrea June* was hanging on by a thread. Judging by the degree of disintegration of the rope, it wouldn't be long before the *Andrea June* broke free and floated out to sea.

"Come on, let's get onboard." Jolene laid the oars on the floor of the dinghy and grabbed the ladder on the side of the boat. Celeste secured the small bottle of lavender oil in her pocket and followed suit, glancing at the dilapidated deck boards dubiously.

"Is that thing going to hold us?" Celeste had visions of plunging through the deck into the waters of the cove below. At least it was warm out and the cove water wasn't that deep.

But the deck held Jolene, so Celeste scrambled onboard behind her.

"Are you sure Mae said you could find the truth here? Maybe there is actually a real person named Andrea June … fishermen name their boats after real people most of the time. Maybe we should be looking for the real Andrea June to find out the truth?"

Jolene shrugged. "Maybe, but I searched all the databases and couldn't find her."

"Now what?" Celeste looked around the small deck. There was nothing really to see—an old moth-eaten life jacket. Half an oar. The old motor hanging off the back was more rust than anything and probably hadn't worked in years.

Jolene pointed toward a small cabin below the deck. "Maybe there will be a clue down there."

Celeste's stomach clenched as she looked into the dark cabin. "Maybe. You go first."

She crowded into the small space behind her sister, propping the cabin door open with a brick that she'd found lying beside it. The cabin consisted of a counter, the remnants of a ratty old mattress and a bucket. Celeste didn't want to speculate as to what the bucket was used for. The dust was an inch thick. No one had been on this boat in years.

Jolene bent over the counter, shuffling through a pile of papers. Celeste planted her feet, steadying herself against the rocking motion of the boat and willing her ears to ignore the alarming creaks and groans.

"Look at this," Jolene said. "These papers are dated the year Mom died."

Celeste bent over Jolene's shoulder to see the seven-year-old newspaper and the breath rushed out of her when she read it. "It's an article about Mom's death."

Jolene looked at her with wide eyes. "Let's see what else is here."

Celeste bent down to help sort through the papers, which included menus, newspaper clippings and some pictures. She stopped short when she came to one that was eerily familiar—the cliff next to their house.

"Why would a picture of our cliff be here?" Jolene mused.

"I don't know, but that looks like the spot where Mom was standing when she ..." Celeste's throat closed up and she let her voice trail off, not wanting to say the words.

"And look at this." Jolene held up a scrap of dark pink silk fabric. Celeste didn't recognize it, but the tone of Jolene's voice made her scalp tingle.

"What is it?"

"I'm not sure, but it looks like a scrap of fabric from the scarf Mom was wearing that day. The one that washed up on the rocks later on."

Celeste stared at the fabric.

Why would fabric from the scarf her mother had worn the day she died be on this boat?

The boat lurched with the force of a large wave and the cabin door swung free of the brick, its rusty hinges screaming with the effort. Celeste lunged forward to catch the door before it slammed shut cutting off the light to the cabin.

She pushed at it and it swung back open. The figure of a man sprang into the doorway, partially blocking the light.

Celeste gasped when she noticed the light filtering through the shadowy figure.

"What is it? Jolene jerked her head in the direction Celeste was looking.

"A ghost," Celeste whispered out of the side of her mouth. Then louder she asked. "Who are you?"

"I'm Barnes. This is my boat and you're trespassing."

"You don't keep your boat up very well," Celeste said. Clearly, he didn't realize he was dead. "Where have you been?"

Barnes' face swirled into a mass of wrinkles. "Been? Why, I been lobstering out at the point."

"The point where our house is?"

"Your house?" Barnes glanced from Celeste to Jolene in confusion. Another wave set the boat rocking. Celeste braced herself on the counter to keep from falling.

"You're those Blackmoore girls? But I thought you were much younger."

"We were back then ..." Celeste's voice trailed off. She realized Barnes' ghost was stuck seven years in the past, but had no idea how to explain it to him.

"What's going on?" Jolene whispered in Celeste's ear.

"It's Barnes, the guy who owns this boat."

"Well then, find out why he has this." Jolene held the scrap of pink fabric up.

"Where'd you get that?" Barnes snarled at Jolene, not realizing she could neither see nor hear him.

"We should ask *you* the same," Celeste said. "It's our mother's, isn't it?

A mix of emotions flitted across Barnes' face. He glanced behind him nervously. Swirls of vapor drifted around him.

"You girls shouldn't be here. It could be dangerous."

No kidding.

"What do you know about our mother?" Celeste persisted. The boat was rocking harder now and an acrid odor drifted past Celeste's nose.

Gasoline?

"I knew your mother. Knew her well. I liked her a lot. That's why I couldn't understand ..." Barnes' ghost shrugged.

"Understand what?" Celeste prompted. "Our mother jumped off the cliff outside our home."

"Is that what you heard?"

"Do you know different?"

"I set my traps out by the cliffs on the south side. I saw your mother on the cliff that evening. "

Celeste's heartbeat picked up a notch. "You did? What did you see?"

Next to her, Jolene was busy swiveling her head between Celeste and the ghost she couldn't see. Celeste sensed the tension coming from her sister. She knew Jolene was dying to find out what they were talking about, but didn't want to interrupt. Barnes was on a roll and Celeste didn't want to stop the interrogation to fill Jolene in.

Barnes glanced behind him again, then his ghostly figure glided a few inches toward them. He lowered his voice. "Let's just say your mother might have had company on the cliff."

Celeste's eyes widened. "Company? Who?"

Barnes glided even closer.

Bang!

The door slammed shut, leaving them in darkness.

"Celeste?" Jolene's shaky voice filled the dark cabin.

"I'm right he—"

Kaboom!

***

Celeste instinctively held her breath as the blast catapulted her into the chilly ocean. She opened her eyes, searching the murky cove waters to get her bearings. Being an experienced scuba diver and accustomed to finding her way under water, it didn't take long for her to figure out which way was up, and she quickly kicked her way to the surface.

She broke through amidst the flaming boat debris. Beads of water flung from her hair as she whipped her head around frantically searching for Jolene.

"Jolene!"

"Over here!" Jolene's head bobbed in the water six feet away and Celeste swam toward it.

Behind them, the dock was a hubbub of activity as people rushed to the dinghies to get into the water and put out the flaming debris before any other boats caught on fire. Two fishermen had jumped in the water and were swimming toward her and Jolene.

"Are you okay?" Celeste came alongside Jolene.

"Yep. But I don't think *Andrea June* is."

Celeste spun around in the water and looked toward the *Andrea June*. Or rather where the Andrea June had once been. Only the deck remained. Partially submerged and slowly sinking. Celeste watched as the bow tipped up higher and higher, while the back of the boat sank lower and lower.

"Are you guys okay?" The two fishermen had reached them. "Can you swim back on your own?"

"I'm okay," Celeste looked at Jolene. "Are you?"

Jolene nodded and the four of them swam to the dock, dodging debris and fishermen rushing out in dinghies on the way. The two men helped pull them out of the water. Someone handed them blankets. Even though it was eighty degrees outside, the ocean water in the cove was only sixties degrees and Celeste was chilled.

"What happened?" someone in the crowd asked.

"Must have been a gas explosion," another answered.

"Whose boat was that?" Celeste heard someone ask behind her.

She turned and recognized the speaker as Bobby Shore, a local.

"Barnes," she answered.

"Barnes?" An older man, Jonathan Wild looked at her strangely. "But, no one has seen him in years."

Celeste shrugged and the harbormaster at the edge of the crowd spoke up. "He hasn't been around, but his mooring fee's been getting paid, so his boat has been sitting all this time."

"If you ask me, its good riddance to that eyesore," someone in the back of the crowd muttered.

"Probably should have gotten rid of that boat long ago. I bet the gas tank was compromised ... it was in such a bad state of repair," a woman said primly.

Celeste and Jolene sat on the edge of the dock and watched while the volunteers put out the rest of the fires, picked planks up from the decks of the other boats and netted the floating debris out of the harbor. It didn't take long for the novelty to wear off and the crowd to disperse.

"What happened back there?" Jolene asked when the onlookers had left them alone on the dock.

Celeste knew she wasn't talking about the explosion. "Barnes' ghost was there. He knew something."

"And those pictures and the scrap of fabric ..." Jolene looked down at her hands. "I dropped it when the boat exploded. We lost that evidence."

"We might have lost the physical evidence on that boat, but now we know you were right about there being more to Mom's death than we were told."

Jolene shrugged. "Well, the pictures and the scarf don't prove much."

"Not that," Celeste said. "The last thing Barnes told me before the boat blew up was that Mom wasn't alone on the cliff the day she died."

Chapter Nine

Jolene's wet clothes felt as heavy as if they were made of lead, but at least they weren't still dripping. The walk home hadn't been pleasant and now, walking up the porch steps, she winced as the soaked jeans chafed her thighs.

"I can't believe no one at the cove saw anyone near the *Andrea June*," Jolene said as she grabbed the front door handle. After the excitement had died down, they'd asked around and no one had noticed anyone anywhere near the boat.

"Do you think it really exploded on its own?" Celeste asked as the two girls headed toward the kitchen where they could take the back stairs upstairs to change.

Jolene made a face. "I doubt it. Too much of a coincidence."

"Well, someone did point out that the neglect might have contributed to it. Maybe conditions were just right and we had bad timing."

Jolene didn't answer. She'd stopped short just inside the kitchen door. On the far side of the room, the door to the basement gaped open ... the girls always kept that door firmly closed.

She glanced quickly at Celeste who was now also staring at the door. She walked slowly over, her heart thudding in her chest as she peered into the dim opening.

"Meow!"

A ghostly face appeared from the depths of the stairs and Jolene sucked in a breath, jumping back as Belladonna trotted into the kitchen with Eliza following behind her.

"Aunt Eliza!"

Eliza looked as startled to see them as they were to see her.

"Oh. Hi. I didn't think anyone else was home." Eliza glanced nervously at the basement door.

Celeste narrowed her eyes at Eliza. "What were you doing in the basement?"

I heard Belladonna crying down there, so I went down to see if she needed help. Thought she might be trapped somewhere." Eliza's brows mashed together as her ice-blue eyes took in first Celeste, then Jolene. "Why are you girls all wet?"

Jolene slid her eyes over to Celeste with a silent warning.

"A boat blew up down at the cove. We jumped in the water to help out." Technically, it wasn't a lie.

"That was nice of you. I hope no one was hurt."

"No, thankfully. Just the boat."

"Well, you girls should get out of those wet clothes. I'm headed into town to visit some old friends. Fiona let me borrow her truck."

"Anyone we know?" Jolene asked.

"I'm sure you probably don't. Just some people I knew way back." Eliza leaned over to snatch Fiona's keys off the counter and fumbled them. They clanked loudly on the floor and she retrieved them, then smiled weakly at the girls and headed down the hall.

"Did she seem nervous to you?" Celeste asked after they'd heard the truck start in the driveway.

"Yeah." Jolene pushed the basement door shut. "And who in their right mind would go in that spooky basement alone?"

"Good question. Our Aunt does seem to have some oddities. Not the least of which is her chosen bedroom."

"Yeah, I always thought that room was creepy."

"Me, too." Celeste glanced down at her clothes. "But she is right about one thing. We need to change."

"Meet me in the east sitting room when you are done. I have something to show you."

Twenty minutes later, Celeste appeared, freshly showered and wearing a white yoga outfit. Jolene was already sitting on the couch in a clean pair of tan capris and navy blue shirt, her laptop open on the coffee table in front of her.

"I wanted to show you this picture taken the night Mom died." Jolene swiveled the computer toward Celeste so she could see the screen.

Celeste bent down and squinted at it. "Is that the cliff?"

"Yes, the very edge where she stood. Look at the footprints."

Celeste's eyes widened. "That's a man's shoe print. But couldn't that have been there before from another day? Or maybe it was from the police attending the scene."

Jolene shrugged. "Maybe. We all know that Overton didn't do a very good job. I wouldn't be surprise if he trampled all over the crime scene. But if what Barnes' ghost told you is true, this could be proof."

"Sure, but what does it really give us? We can't look for someone who wore that shoe. The print could belong to thousands of shoes."

"Right. We have to get more evidence before we tell anyone else what we suspect." Jolene turned the computer back toward her and tapped on the keys.

"What are you doing?" Celeste sank into the chair opposite her.

"Just a little cyber detecting," Jolene said. "We need to find out more about this Barnes guy. Do you remember him at all?"

Celeste shook her head. "No. But if he disappeared a long time ago, I guess I wouldn't."

"Right. Says here that he disappeared three weeks after Mom died." Jolene looked up at Celeste. "That's an odd coincidence ... and whenever there's an odd coincidence, I like to follow the money."

Her fingers flew over the keys as she used her secret—and not entirely legal—software to access the bank database across town. She lucked out on the second try. Barnes still had an account at the Mariner National Bank.

"Ahh ... that explains it," she said.

"Explains what?" Celeste leaned forward, her elbows on her knees.

"Barnes had auto-pay setup in his bank account, so that's how his mooring fees were getting paid. Among other things."

"For seven years? He must have had a bunch of money in there."

Jolene's face scrunched up. "Yeah. It looks like he deposited a lump sum of twenty thousand dollars a few weeks before he went missing. This is getting more and more suspicious."

"Was a big deposit like that unusual?"

Jolene scrolled back through the account. "Yep, it definitely was."

Celeste chewed her bottom lip. "I don't like it. Something was definitely going on. And I could tell Barnes' ghost was scared and he didn't even realize he was dead, which probably means he died suddenly and unexpectedly."

Jolene glanced up again. "Like he was murdered."

Celeste nodded her head slowly.

"I don't see any payments for a mortgage or rent in here which seems odd. I wonder if he still has a house or apartment that we can search. I don't see any mortgage or rent, but there is a payment here for *Birchwood Storage*. Isn't that out on Ledge Road?"

"Yep. Are you thinking he has a storage unit out there still?"

Jolene nodded, her eyes still on the screen.

"You're not thinking about going there and breaking in, are you?"

Jolene nodded again.

"But you don't have a key. How would you get in?"

Jolene glanced up at Celeste and cocked her head to the side. "Really? You're asking me? I am a trained detective, you know, and locks are one of my specialties."

Celeste gnawed on her thumbnail. "I don't like it. This is getting dangerous and I don't think you should go around investigating it on your own."

Jolene felt annoyance bloom in her chest. She hated it when her sisters got all protective of her. She could see why they would have been that way when she was younger, but she was a grown woman now and perfectly capable of taking care of herself ... especially with her special gifts. How many times did she have to prove that to them?

She didn't voice her annoyance, though. She simply said, "You could come with me if you're that worried."

"I'd love to, but I can't." Celeste reached into her pocket and pulled out a small, violet colored bottle. "I managed to save the lavender oil Morgan made for Darlene and I have to drop that off and get to the yoga studio to teach a class by noon."

Jolene simply shrugged and closed the laptop.

"Promise me you won't do anything dangerous like breaking into the storage unit on your own," Celeste said as the two girls stood up.

"I won't do anything I think is dangerous." Jolene figured she was safe in saying that. What

Celeste considered dangerous and what *she* considered dangerous were two different things.

She followed Celeste into the driveway and watched her drive away before starting up her Subaru Brat and taking off in the direction of *Birchwood Storage.*

Chapter Ten

Birchwood Storage was off the beaten path, nestled in a dense, thick stand of pines. A cluster of three birch trees sat out front and Jolene parked behind them and headed toward the office in the small industrial-looking metal building.

Inside, a vaguely familiar incense-like smell hit Jolene's nose. The person behind the desk raised red glassy eyes at her. He had long hair and a ratty t-shirt. Jolene guessed he was still in high school. She smiled to herself. Getting around him would be child's play

"Help you?" he asked and then collapsed into a fit of coughing.

Jolene put on her sweetest face and leaned over the counter.

"My uncle sent me to get something from his unit, but I forgot the number," she giggled coquettishly.

The guy narrowed his eyes at her and tilted his head.

She held up a small key she'd had at the ready. It was the kind of key one used for padlocks. Of course, it didn't go to the padlock for Barnes' storage unit, but the kid didn't need to know that. "I have his key. I just need the unit."

That seemed to satisfy him. He slid the keyboard closer. "What's the name?"

"Gerald Barnes."

He tapped on some keys, squinted at the screen, then looked back at her. "Number three-seventeen. It's all the way in the back."

"Thanks!" Jolene was already out the door and in her car before he could say 'you're welcome'.

Unit three-seventeen was in the last row facing the dense woods. Jolene pulled up in front of it, glad there were no other cars around. She didn't want anyone to see her picking the lock.

She pulled her lock-picking tools out of her purse and got to work. The silence was broken only by the soft click of the metal tools, the chirp of birds and the rustle of squirrels in the woods behind her. The padlock wasn't anything fancy and it only took about five minutes before she had it open and was struggling to push up the rusty metal door, wincing at its screech of protest.

She pushed the stubborn door up only halfway, then ducked under and slipped inside. Daylight filtered in from the partially open door. Specks of dusted floated in the beam of light as Jolene looked around, letting her eyes adjust.

Barnes hadn't kept much in there. A few fishing poles, a pile of lobstering traps, various parts from an old boat. Jolene sighed in disappointment. She was sure there would be a clue in here, but all she could see was old fishing stuff and broken down furniture.

She crossed over to an old empire-style bureau. Its veneer was partially peeled off and it was missing one drawer. Her disappointing search of the other drawers turned up old t-shirts and a bunch of junk drawer stuff.

She puffed out her cheeks and looked around the unit.

Come on clues, where are you?

Suddenly, she remembered an old trick she'd seen on television. She walked to the bureau and started pulling out the drawers, looking on the underside.

She found it under the third drawer. A plain white envelope, yellowed on the edges. She pushed the glue-caked flap open to reveal one photograph inside.

Her heart twisted when she saw her mother's face, the familiar pink silk scarf wrapped around her neck. Johanna looked alarmed and with good reason. The photo showed her being held back (or pushed forward?) by two beefy men. Jolene couldn't make out their faces as they were obscured by the angle of the picture and Johanna being in front. One man had a thick black beard, the other frizzy brown hair. They both had scowls on the parts of their faces she could see. A wide, hairy forearm obscured the foreground of the picture.

The picture had been taken at dusk and she couldn't make out many of the details, but what she could make out froze her blood. From the angle, she could tell it had been taken from the waters below her home with her mother and the men standing on the cliff ... the very spot Johanna had supposedly jumped from.

Jolene's heart raced. This was the proof she'd been looking for.

She backed out of the storage unit, her attention still focused on the picture in her hand. As she started to turn, she felt a prickle at the back of her neck. Her stomach tightened. She ripped her attention from the picture and spun around.

Two dark figures came toward her and she focused on her internal energy, trying to bring it forward to fight them off.

Why couldn't she see their faces? she thought just before she started to feel incredibly sleepy. One of the figures was holding something out toward her—she couldn't quite make out what it was, but she thought it looked like a geode of some sort.

The intense feeling of tiredness overwhelmed her. It felt like someone had pulled a plug and all the energy was draining out of her.

She slumped into a pile on the ground, the picture falling from her fingertips. Her heart sank. She had no idea what these guys were planning, but she was weak as a baby, unable to open her eyes more than a small slit, much less defend herself.

What happened next was a hazy blur. She remembered a lot of shouting and then strong arms picking her up. A faint memory of a familiar face. Mateo. The man she thought she'd seen following her in town.

Then she woke up, the hard, pebble-strewn ground outside the storage unit jabbing painfully into her side and the faint image of Mateo's velvety brown eyes fresh in her memory. He'd saved her once before in a similar situation. Maybe he'd saved her again today. But if so, where was he now?

She shook her head and pushed herself up to a sitting position, scanning the area for enemies.

No one was there.

Did all of that really happen?

The kid in the office was probably too out of it to notice, but did the office have cameras on the units? A quick survey of the corners of the building told her they didn't. No witnesses and nothing recorded on camera. The only evidence Jolene had that something had happened was a stiff neck and aching muscles.

Slowly, she felt her energy return. She stood and brushed herself off. Closing the storage unit, she replaced the padlock and then slid into her car.

It wasn't until she was out of the gate that she realized she no longer had the picture of her mother.

Chapter Eleven

Jolene trudged up the steps to her office, tired and drained. She probably should have gone home to take a nap. Male voices filtered down the stairs from the open office door and she froze in her tracks. Jake and Luke. The last two people she wanted to see.

Jake was supposed to be out in the field and she'd planned to sneak in and get some of her files without having to face him. Luke being with him was even worse. She'd already decided in the car not to tell anyone about the strange incident that seemed more like a dream than reality now, but the two of them had good detecting skills and were bound to figure out something was wrong with her.

She chewed her lip in indecision, then slowly turned, backtracking down to the next step which, unfortunately, chose this time to creak loudly.

"Jolene? Is that you?" Luke poked his head out the door and she was caught. No choice now but to go into the office and pretend like nothing was wrong.

"Hey, Luke. What brings you here?" Jolene asked. "Jake said something the other day about you having another job for us?"

Well, sort of." Luke and Jake exchanged a glance that made Jolene feel uneasy.

91

She tossed her bag on her desk and then sat on it herself, her legs dangling in front. "Oh?"

"Are you okay?" Jake asked.

"Yeah. Just tired. I didn't sleep well last night." Jolene's stomach turned at the lie. She didn't like being dishonest, especially to Jake, but sometimes you had to do what you had to do.

"Oh?" Jake's narrow-eyed study of her told her he didn't fully believe her and she squirmed uncomfortably.

"Anyway," Luke cut in, "my boss has sent a warning. Something's up and you and your sisters are in the middle of it."

Jolene mashed her brows together. "What do you mean by *something*? I thought your company located lost treasure. Why are they interested in four sisters?"

Luke shrugged. Leaning against the wall, he crossed his arms across his muscular chest. "I think they figure you girls are their ace in the hole, what with your gifts and all. They don't want you to get hurt. They need you."

Uneasiness crept into Jolene's gut. She wondered if what Luke was talking about had anything to do with what had happened out at the *Birchwood Storage.*

Should she tell them?

Even though telling them was probably the smart thing to do, she kept quiet. Jolene was fiercely independent and if word got out that she'd been attacked, Luke, Jake and her sisters would start getting overprotective. She didn't need anyone following her every move or restricting her freedom, at least not until she found out the truth about her mother.

"Well, what do they think is going on? Was there some kind of threat? Or does it have something to do with my ancestors' treasure? Are pirates going to descend on us again?" Jolene referred to the incident that brought Luke back to Noquitt in the first place.

Luke had left Noquitt when he was young to join the military. After retiring, he'd taken a job with his current employer, which was a perfect fit for his skills. One of the jobs had led him back here to protect Jolene and her sisters from modern day pirates fixing to steal a treasure her sailing merchant great-great-great-great-grandfather had hidden.

"She didn't say, just that I should protect you guys."

"Protect us?" Jolene snorted. "You've seen us in action—do we need protecting?

Luke's deep green eyes bored into hers. "I can't deny that you guys have the ability to put up a good fight. But have you all been practicing and honing your skills? It seems to me like your gifts are still raw ... if there is a coordinated effort against you, you might not be able to defend yourselves like you think."

Jolene bristled. "We have more control over our gifts now and we *have* been practicing."

It was mostly true. They did practice a little. Okay, maybe not as much as they should, but their paranormal use of energy always seemed to kick in at the right time and had allowed them to escape from danger in the past.

"Another thing I was wondering ..." Luke hesitated, his voice trailing off.

Jolene raised her left brow. "Yeah?"

"How well do you know your Aunt Eliza?"

"I don't know her at all. None of us do. You probably know as much about her as we do at this point."

"Right. Morgan said you guys got a letter out of the blue."

"That's right."

"Have you noticed her doing anything strange?" Luke asked. "I don't mean to imply that she's up to anything ... I mean, I know she's family and all, but it's just that given the warning, I think you guys need to be extra careful."

Jolene thought about her aunt. The truth was, she did get a funny vibe from her, but it wasn't anything she could explain.

Her mind went back to the tour they'd given her on the first day and how it seemed like she was scoping the place out. Almost as if she was looking for something. Then again, maybe she was just sizing the place up to see what everything was worth—after all, she had as much right to the family heirlooms as Jolene and her sisters. And yesterday they'd found her coming up from the basement.

"I'll keep my eye on her," Jolene said. She didn't want to say anything negative about the woman unless she was sure.

"Okay, in the meantime it might be wise for you girls to pair up and make sure you don't go walking around alone." Jake said. "You'll be better able to protect yourselves if two of you are together."

Jolene shot him an angry glare. "Are you serious? I'm not bringing someone around with me all the time. Besides we each have our own businesses that we need to tend to."

"Jo, you know that the people Luke's company deals with are real bad guys. You or your sisters could be hurt, or even killed."

"I know. I'll be careful and I'm sure you guys will make sure Morgan, Fiona and Celeste are protected. But don't forget I'm a trained detective and perfectly capable of handling myself. Plus I have a gun." Jolene patted her purse, then slid off her desk. "And a job to do. So, if you'll excuse me, I'll be on my way. Alone."

Chapter Twelve

Jebediah Powers was scraping barnacles off an old dinghy that rested upside down on two sawhorses when Jolene pulled into his driveway.

"Hey, Jolene. What brings you here?"

"Hi, Jeb." Jolene got out of her car and came to stand beside him. Behind them were deep, dense woods. Jolene glanced into them uneasily, then chastised herself for feeling so skittish. She hoped she wasn't getting paranoid now. "I came about the case you hired Jake and me for. I was wondering if you could tell me more about your traps."

Jeb stopped his work and brushed the back of his hand against his sweaty brow.

"Well, like I told Jake, I drop my traps in the waters just east of the cove opening. Been settin' my pots there for years." A painful look crossed his face.

"Uh huh."

"So, the other day I go out to check 'em and I start pulling up the ropes and the lines are cut on most of the traps."

Jolene knew that lobster traps were set out on a rope that connected them to a buoy. The buoy floated above the water with the trap on the ocean floor. Lobstermen would grab the buoy with a gaffe and pull the trap up on a motorized pulley, then take out the lobsters, keep the ones that were legal size, bait the trap and throw it back in.

"What makes you think Gordy did it, though? Maybe the line just broke," she said.

"The line didn't just break. It was a clean cut. On purpose. Plus I had Billy dive down and all my pots were missin' and most of the buoys were gone, too." Jeb tilted his head and rubbed his chin. "'Course they probably just floated out into the ocean with no traps to anchor them. Someone did it on purpose and Gordy's the most likely suspect on-account-a the feud."

"Yeah, but it seems that's a little drastic, doesn't it? I mean, messing with a guy's lobster traps is against the law. And neither of you ever went that far before, right?" As near as Jolene could remember the Powers-Ellis feud consisted mostly of pranks and practical jokes.

Jeb shook his head. "Nope, we haven't and our daddies never did, either. That's why I'm so mad and I want proof. I lost almost all my traps, and the ones that weren't gone didn't even have any lobsters in 'em … just a weird whale bone."

"Whale bone?"

"Yeah some kind of whale jaw or maybe even a shark. You wanna see?"

"Sure."

She followed Jeb over to a gray shed and watched while he wrestled the door open. He walked a few steps in, then reached up onto a shelf and pulled down a white bone about four inches long, the teeth still embedded.

"You thought this was a whale jaw bone?" Jolene glanced incredulously at Jeb's face as he nodded enthusiastically.

She guessed he had flunked biology in school because it was a plain as day the jawbone she held in her hand wasn't from any fish ... it was from a human.

***

Jeb was more than happy to hand the bone over to Jolene once she convinced him it was from something with two feet instead of two fins. Now, she just had to figure out what to do with it. She didn't want to go back to the office in case Jake and Luke got all overprotective, but she didn't trust the new sheriff, either.

Luckily, she had a friend, Charlene Winters, who was now a rookie at the Noquitt Police Department. She glanced at her watch—she had just enough time to make a quick trip over to Charlene's and still get home early enough to take that much-needed nap before dinner.

Charlene lived in a doublewide mobile home in a well-kept trailer park. As Jolene approached the door, she noticed the mobile home was neat-as-a-pin. Flowers flanked the front in tidy rows and a colorful flag hung from the door. The smell of bacon, onions and beef hit Jolene and her stomach started grumbling as she waited for Charlene to open the door—it had been a long day and she'd forgotten to eat lunch.

"Hey, Jo. What a pleasant surprise." Charlene's flushed face smiled at her from behind the screen door. She wrestled an oven mitt off her hand and pulled the door open.

Jolene gave her old friend a hug, then stepped back to survey the food-stained white bib apron she wore. "Are you cooking something? It smells divine."

"Yes, come on in." Charlene turned from the door and Jolene followed her to the small, bright kitchen. "I'm making beef bourguignon."

"Beef bourguignon? That sounds fancy." Jolene eyed the cluster of pots and pans in the sink. "I didn't know you were a gourmet cook."

Charlene laughed. "Are you kidding? You remember me in high school. I could barely make a peanut butter sandwich. But, once I moved out on my own, I got tired of peanut butter sandwiches pretty quick, so I took a cooking class at the college. It turns out that cooking fancy stuff is pretty easy."

"Really?" Jolene had never thought much about cooking—her sisters always made the meals. Maybe it was time she started pitching in.

"Yeah. I'd invite you to stay, but it won't be ready for another hour."

"That's okay. My aunt is visiting and I should get home to have dinner with her. I just came by for a favor."

"Favor?" Charlene's left brow ticked up.

Jolene grimaced. She hated asking for favors, but she'd taught Charlene to shoot and that had helped her pass the police test, so Charlene owed her. She pulled the bone out of her pocket and held it up.

Charlene gasped. "That's part of a human jaw bone. Where did you get that?"

"Jeb Powers found it in one of his lobster traps."

"Why didn't he bring it to the police?"

"He thought it was a whale bone!"

Charlene's eyes darted to Jolene's face. "You're kidding, right?"

Jolene shrugged. "Nope."

"That's crazy. Whales don't have teeth like that." Charlene took the bone and held it up, studying it from different angles. "It's picked clean. Looks pretty old, too. I wonder how it got in the trap."

"I was wondering that, too. Maybe a lobster pulled it in or it floated in on the current. Anyway, it being there seems to indicate there's a body somewhere out there on the ocean floor."

"It does at that." Charlene said. "You should hand this to the police ... officially, I mean."

Jolene's stomach felt queasy. "I know, but seeing my history with the Noquitt police, I don't really trust them to do the right thing ... and this could be important to me. I'd feel better if you looked into it first."

"Me? Well, I can't really do anything ..."

"Please," Jolene cut in. "My mother died in those waters and her body was never found."

Charlene's face turned sympathetic. Her eyes slid from Jolene to the bone and back again. "So what do you want me to do? Have it tested? I don't know how much I can do without raising a red flag."

"I would be forever grateful if you would try."

"I guess I *do* owe you ..." Charlene took a plastic baggie from a drawer and put the bone in it. "I'll see what I can do without raising suspicions before I hand it over officially ... but I'm not making any promises!"

Chapter Thirteen

Eliza pushed open the front door of the Blackmoore home and cocked her head to listen. The house was quiet, exactly as she'd hoped. She'd gotten her errands done early and even met with a few old friends, just like she'd told her nieces she was going to do ... except these friends weren't ones she wanted her nieces to know anything about.

She knew the sisters worked during the day, which was why she'd rushed home. She had a job to do and it was best if she was left alone in the house to do it.

Glancing back over her shoulder, she frowned at the Subaru parked in the driveway. Jolene's car.

Was Jolene home?

No, the house was too quiet. Jolene and Celeste had probably gone out together in Celeste's car after they dried off from their swim in the cove.

Which made her frown even deeper. Just what *did* happen in the cove? Eliza had gotten a strange vibe from the girls. She knew they weren't telling the truth, but why would they lie?

She didn't have an answer for that and couldn't get sidetracked by trying to figure it out. She closed the door and stepped into the foyer, a hollow longing in her stomach.

It looked almost exactly as it had when she'd lived here.

Childhood memories flooded through her. She and her brother racing down the stairs. Her mother poking her head out of the kitchen to tell them to slow down.

She'd lived in this house until she was twenty years old. Even after her brother had married and moved Johanna in, they'd lived happily here together. Once the kids came, though, she'd moved out on her own to give them some privacy. Still, they'd been close ... until she'd been forced to move.

No one, least of all her mother, had understood why she'd had to leave. Except Johanna. She could still remember the tortured look in her kind amber eyes the day they'd said good-bye.

Eliza took a deep breath. No sense in reliving the past. It couldn't be changed. Letting the breath out in a whoosh of air, she started up the stairs to the third floor.

The third floor of the Blackmoore home was once the servants' quarters back in the day when the family actually *had* servants. Now it was just a warren of rooms and alcoves that were filled with furniture, boxes and miscellaneous 'stuff'. Nine generations of cast-offs were housed in the large space. Some valuable, some not so much.

But one item up here was priceless ... and that was the item Eliza was after.

She stared into the cluttered space, inhaling the smell of old furniture. Dust tickled her nose.

Light filtered through small windows in the dormers scattered along the length of the room. It was stuffy and hot. Eliza moved from the top step into the room.

"Meow!"

Eliza jumped, her shoulders tensing and her heart taking off like a racehorse. Then, her muscles relaxed when she saw the white cat at her feet looking up at her expectantly.

"Jeez, Bella. You spooked me," she whispered, then bent down to pet the cat who responded by rubbing her head against Eliza's calf. A loud purr drifted up, soothing Eliza's nerves.

"So, where is it?" she asked the cat.

As if understanding what Eliza wanted, Belladonna pivoted and flounced down the middle aisle toward the back of the room, where Eliza knew all the really old items were stored— even some things from the original owners, Isaiah and Mariah Blackmoore.

Eliza followed at a more leisurely pace, taking time to look at the old furniture she remembered from her youth. She passed a mahogany marble top dresser with a large mirror in the center. A smile teased the corners of her mouth as she remembered herself as a little girl standing in front of that very mirror with her grandmother behind her, putting her hair in rag curls.

A lot of the furniture that she remembered being in the house when she was little had been moved up here as the family expanded and replaced the old things with newer, modern furniture just as every generation before them had. You could find items lying around or stored in boxes that ranged from twenty to three hundred years old.

Even the books spanned the centuries, Eliza thought, as the bookcase to the right caught her attention. She remembered that bookcase—it was where she'd found Isaiah Blackmoore's journals years ago.

With a start, she realized the books had been disturbed recently. She detoured toward the bookcase, bending down to look at the titles. Someone had definitely been looking at these books—they were all out of order and free from dust. Not only that, but the journals were missing.

She pressed her lips together, a shallow feeling forming in the pit of her stomach. That meant that her nieces had read the journals. She wondered if they had been able to decipher them and how much the girls knew about Isaiah and Mariah Blackmoore and their unusual heritage.

Sighing, she stood up. There was no time for that now. She was on a mission and she'd better complete it before the girls got home.

She made her way out to the center aisle and started toward the back of the attic. Along the way, she stopped to run her fingertips lovingly over the carved mahogany top of a rocking chair that had been her mother's. Her index finger traced the sharp edges of the floral pattern, her heart twisting as she remembered her mother sitting in the chair, rocking her as a child.

"Meow!" Belladonna tore her from her thoughts and she nodded at the cat.

"I know. I have work to do."

Giving the rocking chair one last caress, she ignored the salty tear that slipped from her eye as she followed the insistent cat further into the bowels of the attic.

***

Creak.

Jolene lay in a dinghy staring at the blue sky, listlessly drifting down the river that fed into the ocean at Noquitt beach. Mateo sat on the bench above her. Her guardian angel ... or so she thought. He'd saved her from danger before, but why was he acting so cagey now? She was sure it was him she'd seen near her office, but why would he run?

Creak.

Clouds started to form in the sky above and Jolene suddenly felt cold. She shivered and Mateo looked down at her. But instead of his velvety brown eyes, they were red ... glowing. He reached out toward her and she opened her mouth to scream.

Creak.

Jolene woke in a cold sweat, her heart pounding.

A dream. It was only a dream.

She lay still with her eyes squeezed shut while she waited for her heartbeat to return to normal.

Her eyelids were as heavy as the lead sinkers she used for fishing and it was only a few minutes before she was drifting off to sleep again, the nightmare all but forgotten.

Creak.

What the hell was that noise? She burrowed into the soft bed. Just one more hour of sleep would be perfect.

Creak.

Jolene pushed an annoyed breath out through puffed out cheeks as she flipped on her back, her eyes still shut, willing the annoying noise to stop so she could get some sleep.

Creak.

"Can't a girl get a nap around here!" she shouted into the empty room. She considered pounding on the ceiling to get it to stop, then her eyes flew open wide.

The noise was coming from the attic. Someone was up there.

Who would be in the attic? One of her sisters? Jolene didn't think so. Although they'd made the trip up there on more than one occasion during the past few years, they'd always had a good reason and even though they'd found quite a few treasures up there, the attic still seemed creepy to Jolene.

They'd all been warned by their mother when they were little not to go there, and even though they'd *had* to go up in recent years, they still had an unspoken pact that they'd let the others know if they were going up.

So, it couldn't be one of her sisters. Which left only one other person.

Aunt Eliza.

Jolene reluctantly got out of bed. She was still dressed in her usual outfit of t-shirt and capris. She'd taken off her shoes for her nap, but didn't bother to put them on. It would be easier to sneak up on whoever was in the attic that way.

She made her way to the third floor and started picking her way through the maze of boxes and furniture. The creaking had sounded like it was right above her room, which meant Eliza, or whoever was up there, was in the far corner of the attic.

Her photographic memory had catalogued the areas on the floor that creaked on one of her previous trips up there and she avoided those areas now, moving along silently. Not that she was planning a sneak attack or anything, but if Eliza didn't know anyone else was up there, Jolene might have a better chance of figuring out what she was up to.

Eliza was in the very back of the attic, bent over, her head inside a large box, her silver-white hair hanging down around her like a curtain. Items, presumably discarded from the box, were piled up around her. It was obvious the woman was searching for something.

"Looking for something?" Jolene kept her voice friendly. She wasn't sure what her aunt was up to—maybe she just wanted to look through old family things. Jolene didn't want to jump the gun and accuse her of anything, but her gut instincts told her to remain cautious.

Eliza jerked her head out of the box. Her ice-blue eyes were as large as dinner plates. Her hand flew up to her throat. "You scared the bejesus out of me."

"Sorry, I didn't mean to." Jolene had come up close to the box and she leaned over to peer in. Inside was old clothing—really old. So old that it was deteriorating to dust almost before her eyes. Clutched in Eliza's hand was a cedar trinket box. The cover sat open. It was empty except for the cobalt blue velvet lining inside.

Belladonna came trotting over and started sniffing around the items piled on the floor.

Eliza snapped the box shut and nestled it gently back into the pile of clothing. "I was just rummaging around. I used to come up here a lot when I was a kid. Just stirring up some memories."

Eliza's hawk-like stare unnerved Jolene, making her feel like she was the one being watched—the one that shouldn't have been up there.

"Oh. Mom always warned us about coming up here."

"Mine did, too. But I never listened." Eliza looked around the attic, then back at Jolene. Her eyes softened. "I hope it's not a problem."

"Not at all," Jolene said. "I just heard someone up here and wanted to investigate. This stuff is as much yours as it is ours, really. If you want something, just ask."

Eliza clasped her hands together. "Right. Thanks. Much appreciated."

"No problem." The two women stared at each other awkwardly, then noises drifted up from downstairs.

Eliza cocked her head to the right. "What's that?"

Jolene glanced at her watch. "Must be Morgan and Fiona home from work. We should join them, don't you think?"

Jolene stepped aside and indicated for Eliza to precede her. Eliza smiled and brushed past Jolene. Belladonna trotted past both Jolene and Eliza, taking the lead down the narrow aisle that lead to the stairs.

So much for that afternoon nap, Jolene thought as she followed Eliza down into the kitchen.

Chapter Fourteen

"Were you two up in the attic?" Morgan's forehead creased as she looked between Eliza and Jolene.

"I was just looking around up there," Eliza answered. "So many memories."

"Mew." Belladonna had raced over to her empty food dish, batted it with her paw and sent it skidding across the black and white tile floor.

"Are you hungry?" Fiona looked down at the cat who glanced up at her in disdain as if she was the stupidest creature on the planet. Of *course* she was hungry.

"Right. I'll get your food."

Morgan laughed as Fiona marched straight to the cabinet where they kept Belladonna's food. "We were just going to order pizza. Are you guys in?"

"We are," Celeste and Cal chimed in from the doorway.

"Oh you guys are home." Morgan stated the obvious. "Great."

"I'm in," Jolene said, then turned to Eliza. "What about you?"

"Oh, thanks, but I'm actually meeting someone." Eliza looked at the clock and grimaced. "I better get going. Can I borrow someone's car?"

"Just take my truck." Fiona bent down to pour kibble into Belladonna's dish. "You still have the keys?"

"Yep. Thanks, I really appreciate it." Eliza started toward the front door. "I'll fill up the tank for you."

"Okay. Thanks!" Fiona shouted down the hallway.

The sounds of Fiona's truck starting up drifted into the kitchen and Morgan leaned back to get a clear view of the front door, then said "Does anyone else think it's weird she was in the attic?"

Celeste shrugged. "Kind of, but I guess it makes sense. I mean, this is her family's stuff. She's probably just taking a trip down memory lane."

"True," Jolene said. "She was looking at a box way in the back. The really old stuff."

"That would be the most valuable," Cal cut in. Cal had been a family friend for decades and recently kindled a more intimate relationship with Celeste. He was also an antique expert. His family owned an antiques and pawn shop and the sisters had often used him to evaluate and appraise the various treasures they'd found in the house.

Morgan frowned. "I guess I could see why she'd be interested in that stuff. Our ancestors are her relatives, too. But I have a funny feeling ... especially after what Luke told me today."

"You mean about his boss's warning?" Celeste asked.

"Yep. He stopped by the shop today and told Fiona and me that his boss said we might be in danger and we should be extra careful."

"He stopped by and talked to Jake and me, too. But he was really vague." Jolene said. "Did he tell you anything specific?"

Morgan shook her head. "No, but he's coming by tonight, so maybe he can tell us more."

"Tell you more about what?" Luke asked from the doorway. Luke had practically grown up at the Blackmoore house and had been accustomed to just walking in when they were kids. Even though he'd been away for a long time, old habits were hard to break and he'd been walking in ever since he came back and started dating Morgan again. Jolene loved to tease him about it.

"More about your boss's mysterious warning," Jolene answered, then added. "I must be getting hard of hearing ... I didn't hear you knock.

Luke smirked at her. "I'm afraid I don't know much more about the warning."

"Hey, let's take care of business first." Fiona held her cellphone in her hand, her finger hovering over the number for the pizza place. "What kind of pizza do you guys want? Pepperoni?"

Everyone murmured their assent and she pressed the button and put in the order.

"We should talk about what you girls plan to do to protect yourselves," Cal said, draping his arm around Celeste and pulling her close.

"Do?" Jolene looked at her sisters. "We don't really need to *do* anything. We have skills."

"Yeah, but are you in control of them?" Luke asked

"Sure ... well, I think so." Jolene pressed her lips together. After the sisters had discovered their unusual gifts, they'd made a pact to try to practice and hone them so they'd be able to use them better.

The last time they'd had to defend themselves, the gifts were rather unwieldy and Jolene knew they would have been more effective if they'd been able to harness them properly. They had practiced a little, but then life had gotten in the way and they'd stopped. Jolene knew she could control her paranormal skill better than before, but was it good enough?

The four sisters glanced sheepishly at each other and Jolene knew the other three were thinking the same thoughts. Luckily, they were saved from answering by a knock on the front door.

That's probably Jake," Fiona said, then yelled down the hall. "Come in!"

"At least he knocks," Jolene slid a teasing glance at Luke.

"Anyway, I think it's best if you guys don't go anywhere alone," Luke continued. "We all know your powers are enhanced when you are together."

"What?" Jolene screwed up her face. "That's gonna seriously cramp my style."

"Yeah," Celeste added. "Buddying up might work out okay for Morgan and Fiona since they go to work together anyway, but for Jolene and me, it's just not practical."

"What's not practical?" Jake asked as he sauntered into the kitchen, casting a disappointed glance at the counters. "I thought you said there was going to be pizza?"

"It's on order," Jolene answered. "And what isn't practical is us buddying up and sticking together. We still have our individual jobs to do."

"Oh, you're talking about the warning? What's that really all about?" Jake turned to Luke.

Luke sighed. "All I know is the big boss, Dorian Hall, is very concerned. She's sending some people out to keep an eye on things."

"Sending people out?" Fiona raised a brow. "You mean like last time with those nasty pirates?"

"Yep."

"Great, so we'll have someone watching our every move?" Jolene fisted her hands on her hips. She prided herself on being able to handle her own safety and hated having anyone watch over her.

"If that's what it takes. In fact, she said she's had a few in place for a while and, of course, I'm supposed to keep an eye on you guys, too," Luke winked at Morgan who look more annoyed than pleased.

So, someone has *been watching me*, Jolene thought.

But they weren't doing a very good job if those guys had gotten to her at the storage facility. She wondered if those were the 'bad guys' Luke was talking about and, if so, why had they let her go? She debated mentioning it, but decided against it —if Luke and Jake knew, they might insist on making sure none of them went anywhere alone.

"Well, great then. If someone is watching us, we don't need to buddy up," Jolene said hopefully.

"I think you still should," Luke said. "If Dorian is involved, that means it's serious and whoever is behind this is ruthless. They'll stop at nothing to get what they what. Whatever that is."

Jolene frowned. "Good question. What *do* they want?"

Luke shrugged and spread his hands at his sides. "Dorian was pretty vague about that."

Jolene had no idea what this evil person might want. She wondered if the attack at the storage place and on Barnes' boat had anything to do with it. Glancing at Celeste out of the corner of her eye, she could see her sister was thinking the same thing about Barnes' boat. Jolene gave her head a subtle shake. She didn't want to tell the others lest it restrict their freedom even more.

Celeste gave a slight nod in return and Jolene relaxed, knowing her sister understood and agreed not to tell.

"So, you think this person could be more ruthless than Goldlinger?" Fiona asked, referring to the maniacal thug who had descended on them to try to steal a three-hundred-year-old treasure dating back to the time of Isaiah Blackmoore.

The treasure had been hidden on their property unbeknownst to the Blackmoore sisters and the girls had almost been killed defending it. In the end, they'd had to summon the forces of their powers to defeat Goldlinger's henchmen. That's when they'd learned the true power of their gifts.

Luke shrugged. "Yep. This guy is even more powerful and even more of a badass. In fact, our sources tell us Goldlinger is just one of his henchmen."

"So, are they after treasure again? Or something else they think we have?" Jolene glanced up at the attic thinking about the journals they'd discovered that had led them to the treasure.

Was that what Eliza had been looking for?

They'd never fully deciphered all of the journals—maybe there was more in there and that's what this guy was after.

"I'm not sure. I get the impression it's more personal than that."

"Personal?" Celeste asked.

"Yes. So there is an immediate threat to you girls. And you probably can't trust anyone," Luke answered.

"Which brings me to your Aunt Eliza," Jake cut in. "What do you girls really know about her?"

"What are trying to say?" Morgan shrugged one shoulder, a sour look on her face. "She's our *aunt*. She got into some kind of fight and left a long time ago and is now back for a visit."

"Why come back now?" Jake asked. "It seems like strange timing is all I'm saying. An odd coincidence she'd appear out of nowhere and insinuate herself in the house when there is a threat against you girls. And in my line of business, there's no such thing as coincidence."

"Maybe you should do a little investigating on her," Luke suggested.

"Investigate our aunt?" Celeste bristled. "That doesn't seem right. She's a Blackmoore and we don't investigate our own people."

"But aren't you the least bit curious as to why she left and what she's been doing all this time?" Jake asked.

"Maybe." Celeste pressed her lips together. "But that still doesn't mean I condone investigating *family*."

The arrival of the pizza suspended the conversation and they all took a gooey slice and sat around the kitchen island with paper plates and a roll of paper towels.

Jolene picked a pepperoni off her slice and popped it into her mouth. The salty grease tickled her taste buds. They ate in silence for a few minutes, the only sounds an occasional nummy noise.

"So where *is* Eliza tonight?" Jake asked as he picked out his second piece of pizza.

"She said she was going to visit friends," Jolene answered.

Jake raised a brow. "Really? Did she say who?"

"No," Morgan cut in. "And we weren't about to give her the third degree."

"Of course not. It just seems funny that after being gone for twenty years without contacting any of you, she'd still have friends back here."

Jake had a point. Eliza sure did seem to have a lot of people to visit in town and she never once mentioned who any of them were.

Jolene looked around the kitchen at her family. A feeling of foreboding spread in her stomach, making the pizza weigh heavy. Usually it was Morgan who had the premonitions, but tonight, Jolene had one herself.

Shoving aside her plate, she swallowed hard, trying to push down the lump that was forming in her throat as she wondered if this might be their last supper together.

***

Eliza Blackmoore pulled the key out of the old truck's ignition and listened to the engine sputter out. Clicking off the lights, she stared into the depths of the darkened woods. It was dusk and the dense forest was cloaked in shadow.

She'd better hurry. Soon it would be totally dark.

Eliza hurried down the path, the dark trees looming beside her like silent sentinels. The hazy dusk gave the woods a dream-like quality. The forest was almost silent except for the sound of her own heartbeat and a few birds letting out their last chirps before bedding down for the night. To her left, a chipmunk rustled in the dried leaves on the forest floor, pulling her startled attention away from the path.

When she looked back at the path, a dark figure stood just ahead.

"Did you find it?" the woman whispered as Eliza drew closer.

Eliza sighed, her heart sinking. She hung her head. "No."

A pale, wrinkled hand reached out and tilted her chin up so she was looking into the clear amber eyes of the old woman. Her skin was as pale as centuries-old parchment, which made her eyes appear to glow with an ethereal light.

Or maybe they really *were* glowing?

No, it's probably just a trick of the lighting, Eliza thought as she studied the small woman in front of her. She was dressed in a long black cloak, the hood pulled up over her silver hair, making her small face appear to float inside its dark shadow.

Eliza looked into her eyes, but instead of the disappointment she expected to see, she saw only understanding and wisdom.

"Never fear. I know you will succeed."

"I think I know where to look. I got close today, but was interrupted."

"It's critical you find it, or all may be lost. It could be the difference that keeps our opposers from gaining the upper hand."

"I know." Eliza felt the weight of the world on her shoulders. "I still have a few places to look."

The woman nodded, pulling her cloak closer as a breeze kicked up the dried leaves on the path causing them to swirl around their feet. "You must be alert. I feel the wind of change is close."

"I will."

"Good, then." The amber eyes narrowed. "And what of the girls?"

"They seem to be virtually unaware."

The woman simply nodded. Lowering her voice she said, "Don't forget your mission—more than one life hangs in the balance."

And then she stepped backward and turned, melting into the shadows of the trees. Eliza stood there blinking at the empty forest.

Had the woman vanished into thin air?

No, it probably just *seemed* that way. Night had fallen and Eliza could barely see more than ten feet in front of her. The old woman had simply walked out of her line of vision.

Eliza turned, her stomach jittery with nerves, wondering if she'd be able to make her way back to the truck now that it was dark. As if by divine intervention, the three-quarter moon appeared from behind the long thin cloud that had been hiding it, illuminating the woods enough for Eliza to see the path in front of her.

She started back toward the parking lot, sucking in a startled breath when something appeared directly in front of her.

A deer blinked at her with its large eyes. Its dark, velvety nose twitched. Eliza could hear it exhaling puffs of breath as the two stood frozen, staring at each other. Then it turned and silently bounded off into the woods.

Eliza quickened her pace. She had to get back home and find what she'd come to find before things turned for the worse. She wondered how much she should tell her nieces.

How much did they know already?

She had no idea, but if she had to lie to them, then so be it. Her mission was most important. She'd left town for a good reason all those years ago, and she wasn't about to let all that sacrifice be for nothing.

Chapter Fifteen

Jolene and her sisters had given in to Luke, Jake and Cal's pleas for them to 'buddy up'. So, the next day, Fiona and Morgan went to *Sticks and Stones* together, as usual, which left Jolene and Celeste to keep each other out of trouble.

Since Celeste didn't have to work until later that day, she accompanied Jolene on her stakeout of Gail. Jolene usually preferred to work alone, but at least bringing Celeste along was better than having to drag Jake, Luke or one of Luke's minions with her.

A lot of the work Jolene did involved sitting in her car waiting for someone to go somewhere so she could follow them. She had to admit, it could get kind of boring, so having Celeste along today wasn't that objectionable.

"Eliza sure spends a lot of time in her room," Celeste said as they sat in the Subaru along a side street near Gail and Steve's house. "I pictured that she'd be doing more stuff with us."

"Maybe she's a loner and likes to keep to herself." *Like me.*

"Maybe. We have been busy, too, and we do spend all day at work. I'd just like to get to know her better."

"Maybe we can plan something for all of us to do together this weekend," Jolene offered.

"Good idea."

"Here she comes." Jolene kept her eyes on the side mirror where she had spotted Gail's green Subaru motoring down the street toward them. She waited for it to go by, then pulled out a few seconds later. "The key is to follow along behind, but not so close so that the person suspects they are being followed."

"Hopefully she won't be looking for anyone tailing her," Celeste said. "Do you expect her to be up to something?"

"Yep. Steve said he heard her make a date for this afternoon."

"Oh. Gosh, that's terrible. He must feel awful." Celeste stared out the window. "I don't know how you can do this job sometimes."

Jolene shrugged. "It's not bad all the time. Besides, someone has to do it. I'm just sorry you have to tag along. It's probably boring for you."

"Well, I like the company." Celeste smiled. "I just wish Luke would give us more information. The place he works for can't really be keeping him as much in the dark as he pretends."

"You think he's holding back on us?" Jolene asked. She hadn't considered that. But why would he?

"I don't know. The whole thing is strange."

Up ahead, Gail pulled off onto a less traveled street and Jolene slowed down so that she wouldn't be too close before she took the same turn. She glanced uneasily in her rear-view mirror after she turned down the road.

"Is someone following us?" Celeste half turned in her seat to look out the back.

"No. I don't think so. I'm just nervous about it, I guess. Luke has me all spooked now." Jolene didn't mention the part about getting knocked out at the storage facility—no sense in getting Celeste all worried.

"Have you found out anything more about Mom?" Celeste's tentative voice at the mention of their mother made Jolene's stomach lurch.

"Well, I'm not sure if it's about Mom, but I did find something strange at Jeb's the other day."

"At Jebs?"

"Yeah. I was out there asking about the traps that he thought Gordy had taken and he showed me something he found in one of the remaining traps. He thought it was a whale jaw, but it was a human jaw!"

"What? Gross." Celeste scrunched her face up and then her eyes widened. "And you think it might be from ..."

"Her body was never found," Jolene cut in so her sister didn't have to say the words.

"Oh." Celeste stared out the side window and the two girls fell silent as Jolene followed Gail further into the boonies.

"Where the heck is she going?" Celeste said after a few minutes.

"Maybe to some out-of-the-way motel?" Jolene felt her heart sinking for Steve. It looked like he was right. She was off to meet her lover at some remote destination.

"I don't know of any motel down here," Celeste said as they watched Gail pull off onto a narrow dirt road.

"You know all the motels in the area?" Jolene raised a brow at her sister and pulled over. It would be too obvious if she followed Gail down that narrow road. "What do you think is down there? It looks almost like it could be a driveway."

"You never know out here." Celeste opened her window and craned her neck to see down the road. "I think there is a mobile home at the end."

"That's weird. Maybe that's where the professor lives." Jolene reached into the back seat and pulled out her camera and telephoto lens. "Come on, let's go see what she's up to."

The two girls closed their car doors softly and crept through the woods, taking care to stay off the road and out of sight of the house. They hid behind a large bush about two hundred feet from the well-kept mobile home.

"What are all those cars?" Celeste pointed to the yard where six cars were parked at various angles. "If she was meeting him for an affair wouldn't there be only one other car?"

Jolene brought the camera up to her face and aimed it at the mobile home. "Maybe it's some kind of swingers club or something?"

"Wait. I think I see movement in the living room," Celeste said.

"They left the curtains open?" Jolene focused the lens so that she could see straight into the living room, gasping as she scanned the group of people, recognizing some of the objects she saw in their hands.

"What is it?" Celeste danced on her tiptoes squinting with her hand shading her eyes trying to see all the way to the mobile home.

Jolene snapped a few shots as proof for Steve, then handed the camera to her sister. "Look for yourself. You won't believe it."

Celeste grabbed the camera and plastered it to her face, adjusting the lens. Then Jolene heard her breath whoosh out. She lowered the camera and stared at Jolene. "A Pampered Chef party?"

Jolene shrugged and the girls giggled as they turned to go back to the car. "I'm kind of glad we didn't catch Gail doing anything. I hate to have to be the one to give Steve the bad news. He's really stuck on her."

"Hmmm..." Celeste's distracted nod set Jolene's nerves on edge. Celeste was looking to the left, scanning the woods. Jolene squinted in that direction. The hairs on her neck tingled.

Someone was out there. Watching them.

She turned her head forward and kept walking, focusing on the energy of whoever was watching, honing her senses like a torpedo zeroing in on an enemy vessel. Then suddenly she turned and thrust her palm out in the direction where she thought the watcher was.

A ball of bright blue electricity shot out of her hand, zinging through the woods and crackling against a tree. Sparks flew out, falling to the ground like the sparkles of a firecracker. The electricity was a little off target and a lot stronger than Jolene had intended—maybe she *should* have been trying harder to hone her skills.

"Jeez, I guess you've been practicing." Celeste's face was pale. "Was someone out there?"

Jolene frowned into the woods. "I'm not sure. I *felt* like someone was, but I didn't hear a yell and don't see anyone running."

"Maybe you missed."

Jolene scowled at her sister and Celeste laughed.

"Anyway, the important thing is that you have been practicing and you can fend off a bad guy. Luke and Jake were worrying for nothing ... at least about you." Celeste glanced around uneasily. "My skills seem to be more geared toward the energy of the past. I don't really have any paranormal ability to defend myself."

"Aww, don't worry, sis." Jolene put her arm around Celeste. "I'll protect you."

She was rewarded with Celeste's warm smile. "I appreciate that. But what am I going to do when you're not around?"

***

Jolene dropped Celeste off at her yoga studio. Cal would pick Celeste up after work and bring her home, which was where Jolene was supposed to go now as Luke had some of his minions watching the house to make sure nothing bad happened.

She had no idea what *bad* thing they thought was going to happen, but she wasn't too worried.

She'd proven in the woods that she could take care of herself, even if her intensity and aim was a little bit off.

On the way home, she decided to stop at the bakery in Noquitt Center and get one of her favorite blueberry muffins—the kind with giant plump berries and crunchy crystals of sugar on top.

It was a bright sunny day in the mid-eighties and Noquitt Center was crowded with tourists in bright colors and noisy flip-flops. They strolled along the streets eating ice cream, lugging beach bags and taking up all the parking spots. Jolene had to park a few blocks away, but she didn't mind. The walk would do her good.

As she walked, she let her gifts take over and scanned the crowd from a paranormal perspective. The auras were mostly happy. The center of town was filled with vacationers who weren't paying the least bit of attention to her. She wondered if there was someone in the crowd who was watching her, but she couldn't tell from any of the energy signals she was feeling.

She wasn't too worried about it, either. What could "they" do in a crowded downtown area? It's not like someone could rush into the street and grab her without being noticed. This was probably the safest place for her.

"Jolene!"

She heard her name being shouted from the right and spun around to see Steve Flint sitting on a bench. His clothing was rumpled, his face lined with worry.

"Hi Steve." She walked over and stood in front of him.

"Did you find anything about ..." He let his voice trail off, but Jolene knew what he meant. She could feel the anxious energy coming off him in waves and she stepped back a bit.

"Well, as a matter of fact, I did find something."

Steve's face crumbled. He slouched back in the chair. "I knew it."

"But, it's not what you think."

His forehead wrinkled and he squinted up at her. "What?"

"I did follow Gail earlier today like you asked, but she didn't go to meet her lover ... she went to a Pampered Chef party."

"Pampered Chef? What the heck is that?"

"Oh, you know, it's when a bunch of girls get together to chat and buy expensive items. They have parties for jewelry, makeup and so on. The Pampered Chef one is for kitchen items."

Steve looked perplexed. "Kitchen items? But Gail barely steps foot in the kitchen."

"Well, my guess is that most of the people go to these parties for the gossip. That, and to help their friend get enough hostess points to collect a bunch of freebies." Jolene had little use for these types of parties and always dreaded being invited. She usually showed up late, left early and bought the least expensive item.

Instead of looking happy, Steve looked more worried than before. Jolene noticed how gaunt and pale his face was. *This thing is really taking a toll on him*, she thought.

"I just wish you could get some proof so this whole thing would be over. It's killing me." His pleading eyes looked up at her and her heart twisted.

"I know. I'll try harder," she promised. "I'll have something concrete for you by the end of the week."

"Okay. Thanks." Steve leaned back in the chair and his eyes took on a faraway look. "We'll talk later."

"Okay. Bye." Jolene continued to the bakery, the thought of the plump blueberry muffin not seeming quite so sweet anymore.

Chapter Sixteen

Morgan and Fiona were having a conversation similar to the one Jolene and Celeste had had about their Aunt Eliza as they worked on their separate projects at *Sticks and Stones*.

"There's something kind of strange about her, don't you think?" Morgan asked as she pinched some dried herbs from a container and crumbled them into the bottom of a stone mortar.

Fiona shrugged, holding a pink tourmaline earring up to the window so that the light filtered through it like stained glass. "I guess so. But maybe she's just nervous being around us or something."

"Not too nervous to go skulking around in the attic, though."

"True. And she hasn't been around that much. Like Jake said, how many friends can she still have in Noquitt? She's been gone a long time."

"Good point. But we really should try to spend more time with her. She seemed nice the first night when we all had supper together. Maybe she'll be around for supper tonight."

The bells over the door chimed, causing the girls to look up from their work.

An old woman stood in the doorway silhouetted by the sunlight streaming in behind her. She must have been ninety if she was a day. Her skin was pale, almost translucent like tissue paper.

She paused uncertainly in the doorway, holding something in her hand—a piece of jewelry, it looked like. Morgan knew right away this was no ordinary piece.

"Can we help you?" Morgan asked, unable to take her eyes off the unusual piece of jewelry.

"Yes, I hope so." In contrast to her appearance, the woman's voice was strong with a slight lilt to it.

She walked over to Morgan, still holding out the jewelry, which Morgan could now see was a locket.

Fiona must have seen it, too, from her workbench on the other side of the shop, because she appeared next to the woman, bending her head down to look at the piece that she had placed on the counter.

"This was my grandmother's." The woman said. "Passed down through the family, but as you can see it's got some damage."

The locket appeared to be ancient. It was made from the strangest material Morgan had ever seen. It appeared to be some sort of stone with geometric striations through it. The sides and edges were decorated with delicate gold filigree and a small garnet set in a filigree frame glowed from the middle.

"It's beautiful," Fiona said.

Morgan reached out to re-position the locket so she could see it. As she touched it, she felt a surge of energy.

She gasped pulling her hand back and looked up at the woman who was assessing her with clear, amber-colored eyes. Morgan had the fleeting feeling that this was about more than just fixing a locket.

She cleared her throat and turned to get one of the contact forms the girls kept behind the desk.

"If you can just fill this out, we'll take a look." She turned to Fiona who seemed to be mesmerized by the necklace. "Do you think you can fix it, Fi?"

"What?" Fiona looked up, apparently startled by the question. "Yes, of course."

"It's very unusual," Morgan said. "Do you know anything about it?"

The woman glanced up from the form she was filling out. "Just that it's very old. My grandmother always wore it and after she died I kind of lost track of it. I just found it in the attic with some of her old things yesterday."

"It's some sort of crystal or stone ... but I don't know what it is." Fiona's eyes were still glued to the locket.

The woman put the pen down and pushed the form to Morgan. "Well, that should do it. Do you need anything else?"

Morgan glanced at the form. "Nope. We'll call when it's ready."

The woman turned and headed to the door. Pausing with her hand on the knob, she looked back at them. "Take good care of it, it could be more important than you think."

Morgan's brow creased, thinking that was an odd thing to say, but when she looked up to ask the woman what she meant, she was already gone, the shop door firmly shut even though Morgan couldn't recall hearing the bell.

"I've never seen a stone like this." Fiona dangled the locket in front of her watching it twirl at the end of the gold chain. "It's not really that pretty of a stone, but unusual enough to be interesting."

"The garnet and filigree help, though," Morgan said.

"Definitely." Fiona put it back on the counter and slipped her fingernail under the edge of one of the broken sections of filigree. "It will be no easy task to match this fine work."

Morgan put her fingers gently on the locket to turn it to face her. Her fingertips tingled and she felt a surge of something go through her. Power? Energy? She pulled her hand away.

"What is it?" Fiona looked concerned.

"When I touched it ... it felt strange."

Fiona hovered tentative fingers over the locket, then cautiously rested them on top of it. Her eyes widened and she looked at Morgan. "It feels tingly. I feel energized. Like the stone is giving me energy or something."

"That's how I felt!" Morgan looked down at the locket. "We should find out what's inside this thing."

Fiona picked the locket up to inspect the hinge. "The hinge looks okay. I wonder why it won't open."

Turning the other side to face her, she gently pushed on the clasp but it appeared to be wedged stuck.

"Hmmm ... that's strange." Fiona took the locket over to her worktable. "Let's see what I have here that might help..."

She rummaged through the tools, coming up with a thin dental pick and very carefully put the tip into the locket near the clasp and moved it ever so slightly to pry the locket open.

A bolt of electricity shot out of the locket, zinged across the room and incinerated a wooden side table in a puff of smoke. The cut crystal vase full of fresh cut roses that had been on the table hovered in the air for a split second before crashing to the floor in a watery mess of glass shards and petals.

Fiona and Morgan gaped at the mess.

"Wow. That sure isn't any ordinary locket," Morgan said.

Chapter Seventeen

Jolene started her car and pulled off the top part off her blueberry muffin before edging out into the traffic.

Biting into the muffin top, she felt the satisfying crunch of the large sugar granules that were sprinkled liberally on top as the carbs raced through her bloodstream, making a bee-line to her brain.

She needed the sugar from the muffin to maneuver her way around the downtown Noquitt traffic. It was tourist traffic, and tourist traffic wasn't like regular traffic because they tended to slow down to gawk at shops, scenic views and even other tourists. Tourist traffic was also known to suddenly stop without warning. One needed to have their wits about them to navigate it successfully and, for Jolene, sugar usually did the trick.

As she worked her way out of Noquitt Center toward Perkins Cove, her mind turned to Steve and Gail Flint. She felt terrible for Steve but she also wondered if he wasn't being a bit paranoid. She hadn't seen any indication that Gail was cheating and she was pretty good at picking up on these things.

But, if she wasn't cheating, why all the secret phone conversations and clandestine meetings?

Her chirping phone drew her attention to the passenger seat, her mind already deciding she would ignore it if it were Luke, Jake or one of her sisters calling to check up on her.

It wasn't. It was Charlene. Jolene tensed, thinking of the jawbone she'd left with her friend —she wasn't sure if she was ready to hear the answer. The muffin she'd just swallowed formed a lump in her throat.

"Hi, Charlene."

"Hey, Jo. I have some news about that bone you gave me."

"Uh huh."

"I was able to get a dental match on it."

"And ..."

"It's not your Mom's."

"What?" Jolene hadn't realized she'd been holding her breath, but now it rushed out. She didn't know if she felt relieved or disappointed.

"It belongs to some guy named Barnes."

"Gerald Barnes?" Images of the cabin of the old boat and then the explosion in Perkins Cove flitted through her mind. "That's the old fisherman who's been missing."

"I know. I did some research," Charlene said. "I called in a favor from a friend for the dental match so it's all been done unofficially like you wanted. But now that I know it could help on the missing person's case, I need to submit it through proper channels."

"That's okay." Jolene said. "I appreciate you doing it on the down low."

"No problem." Charlene clicked off.

Jolene frowned as she tossed the phone on the seat. It wasn't really a surprise that Barnes was dead. After all, they'd talked to his ghost. But what she couldn't figure out was what his body was doing out in the ocean. If he'd been out fishing and fallen overboard, that would make sense. But, if that were the case, his boat would have been adrift in the ocean, not moored in his spot in the cove. Something didn't add up.

Charlene had taken a risk getting that information on the sly and Jolene felt like she owed her. She wanted to do something to show her appreciation, but what?

Her thoughts went back to the beef dish Charlene had been cooking and then flitted to the Pampered Chef party. Maybe Charlene would appreciate something for the kitchen. She'd heard Pampered Chef had the best of the best.

And then a thought struck her like a lightning bolt.

She stomped on the brake pedal and cut the wheel to take a sharp right. Ignoring the honking horns and screeching brakes behind her, she turned onto the side road that doubled back toward the center of town.

Sure, she was *supposed* to be heading straight home, but she had an idea that might help prove her case and she *had* to act on it. And besides, what could possibly happen to her in broad daylight?

***

Morgan pulled her Toyota into a spot across from *Reed Pawn and Antiques* and peered through her side window into the shop.

"It looks like he doesn't have any customers," Fiona said as the two girls exited the car and waited for traffic to pass so they could cross the street.

"Good. The less people that see this," Morgan pointed to the white paper bag where she carried the locket, "the better."

Fiona nodded. The traffic broke and they sprinted across, pulling open the door and spilling into the shop.

Cal Reed stood, leaning with his palms on the display case he used as a counter in front of him, studying a book that lay open on the top of the glass. He looked up and smiled at them, his dimples and sparkling blue eyes highlighting his boyish good looks.

It was easy to see why Celeste had fallen for him. Morgan just wondered why it had taken her sister so darn long. Cal and Celeste had been best friends since grade school and Cal was almost like a brother to Morgan, Fiona and Jolene who all knew years ago that the two were perfect for each other. But, for some reason, Cal and Celeste hadn't figured that out themselves until a couple of years ago.

"So let's see this magic locket." Cal held out his hand and Morgan took the locket out of the white bag, gently placing it in Cal's palm.

Cal's eyes widened. "Well, that certainly is unusual." He turned it over in his palm, then held it closer to his face, studying it from every angle. Then he took a loupe out of his pocket and studied it again.

Morgan and Fiona stood patiently watching. Morgan noticed that Cal hadn't said anything about handling the locket making his fingers tingle or getting a rush of energy. Maybe that was a one-time thing ... or maybe it only happened to her and Fiona. Cal didn't have any 'gifts'. Maybe the locket only affected people that did.

Cal took the locket over to the book he had been reading and bent over it looking from the page to the locket and back again. He flipped to the next page and repeated the process.

Morgan stood beside him, peeking over his shoulder.

"I'd say this locket is made mostly of meteorite." He straightened and looked at the girls.

Fiona's brows snapped into a 'V'. "Meteorite? Like from outer space?"

"Yep."

"But those are just ugly rocks," Morgan said.

"Unless you cut them and polish them same as any other rock or crystal." Cal pointed to the locket. "See these lines—how they create a geometric pattern?"

The girls nodded.

"Look at this picture of a cut meteorite." Cal pointed to a picture in the book, which showed a large rock that had been cut in half exposing the inside. Sure enough, the markings were strikingly similar to the locket.

"I guess it's the same as any gemstone," Fiona said. "When they come out of the ground, they usually don't look that great, but once they are cut and polished you see their true beauty."

"Sure, but the end result isn't really that pretty," Morgan pointed out as she looked at the dull gray locket.

"The pattern is interesting." Cal said. "And ancient civilizations thought meteorites had special powers because they came streaking down from the sky."

"Is the locket that old?" Fiona asked.

"Well, I wouldn't say it's ancient, but it could be three or four hundred years old. It's well made. Probably cost a pretty penny." Cal looked up at Morgan. "Did you say the lady's phone was out of order?"

"Yep." Morgan had tried to call her after the locket had incinerated their table, but her number had been disconnected, which was odd since she'd just filled out the form that morning.

"Maybe we can have Jolene google her or something," Cal suggested. "I'd love to talk to her and find out more about it. It's quite unusual."

"You can say that again," Fiona said.

Cal glanced out the window to make sure no one was about to come into the shop. "Did you say it shot out electricity when you tried to open it?"

Fiona and Morgan nodded solemnly. Cal knew about the girls' special gifts and had even witnessed them in action more than once, so they weren't afraid he'd think they were nuts. Anyone else would, though, so it was a good thing they were alone in the shop.

Cal pushed the clasp.

Morgan wasn't surprised when it didn't open.

He pushed harder trying to wedge his thumbnail into the opening to pry it.

Nothing.

"I wouldn't try to force it unless you want your shop to go up in flames," Fiona warned.

But he did try. And still nothing happened.

"I don't see any electricity shooting out," Cal said.

Morgan frowned at the locket. "Maybe we used it up."

"Or maybe it only happens to people who are paranormally inclined," Fiona suggested.

"Do your fingertips tingle when you touch the stone?" Morgan asked.

Cal pressed on the stone with his index finger. "No."

"Mine did."

"Mine, too," Fiona chimed in. She touched the stone, then pulled her fingers back quickly as if stung. "Still do."

Cal flipped to a page he'd marked in the book. "It says here some ancient cultures believed meteorites could amplify energy."

"Maybe that's what it's doing to us," Morgan said. "Amplifying our energy ... our gifts. That's why our fingers tingle."

"Maybe," Fiona said. "Now we really need to talk to Mamie Green and find out more."

"She might not know any more. Remember she said she remembered seeing her grandmother wear it, but hadn't seen it in years until she came across it in her grandmother's things."

"True, but it's worth a try," Fiona said. "I'm dying to find out what's inside it, but I don't want to force it open and break it. Or burn something down. I am supposed to be *fixing* it, not destroying it."

"I'd like to know more, too." Cal looked at the clock over the door. "But right now I have to go pick up Celeste. Maybe we can research it some more back at your place tonight. Jolene will be there to help us. She's such a wiz on the computer."

"That sounds good." Morgan let him usher them toward the door. "But let's not say anything in front of Eliza. I have a funny feeling about her, and with everything going on now I'm not sure how much we want to let her know about us."

"So you think we can't trust her?" Cal asked. "Maybe she shouldn't be at your house. Do you think she could be part of the threat Luke's been talking about?"

Morgan shrugged. "I'm not sure, but until we know more about either Eliza or the threat, the less information we give away, the better."

***

Eliza Blackmoore stomped down the attic steps in frustration. She'd scoured all the older boxes and still didn't find what she was looking for.

It *had* to be here somewhere.

She turned in a slow circle on the second floor landing. Squeezing her eyes shut, she willed her senses to ferret out the item and point her in the right direction.

She needed a sign—her nieces would be home soon and that would really put a damper on her searching activities.

"Meow!"

Eliza's eyes flew open and zeroed in on Belladonna, who sat at the bottom of the stairs staring up at her with those ice-blue eyes.

Was this the sign she'd been asking for?

"Hey, Belladonna. Do you have a message for me?"

The cat stared at her lazily, then winked one eye.

Eliza started down the stairs and Belladonna trotted off in the direction of the kitchen. Eliza's stomach fluttered with excitement as she followed the cat into the kitchen, but her excitement was squelched when Belladonna stopped next to her food bowl and looked from the bowl to Eliza pointedly.

"Oh, is that it? You just wanted me to feed you?"

Belladonna answered by pushing the bowl toward Eliza.

Eliza sighed and went to the cabinet where she'd seen Fiona put the cat food. Taking down the bag, she crossed to the cat bowl, poured some in and started back to return the bag.

The door to the cellar caught her eye as she turned. Her previous exploration of the cellar had been cut short when Jolene and Celeste had come home soaking wet the other day. Now was the perfect time to continue.

She quickly put the cat food back, then slipped her hand inside the door and flipped the switch that lit the low wattage bulb that provided the only source of light in the basement.

Pulling the door all the way open, she grimaced at the hinges' squeal of protest. Good thing she was the only one home to hear it.

She started down the steps, feeling a chill as she got closer to the bottom. The damp smell of mildew tickled her nostrils. She stepped onto the packed dirt floor and turned to the left.

The cellar was empty except for a few piles of junk in the far end. She'd already searched the junk, but there was one interesting piece she hadn't had time to play around with.

The giant wine cask sat against the wall looking totally out of place in the dank basement. It was almost six feet tall and the old convex oak boards were dark with age. Bands of copper and copper rivets still held it together as they had hundreds of years ago.

It would be more appropriate in a winery, Eliza thought, as she walked toward the ancient looking piece.

Could it be a leftover from Isaiah Blackmoore's travels?

If so, it would have been here when Eliza lived here and she didn't remember it. Of course, that wasn't saying much—she hadn't come down in the basement often, and back then it had been crammed full of stuff so the cask probably would have been invisible behind all the junk.

As she approached the cask, she felt a funny sensation like a humming inside her body. She closed her eyes and inhaled deeply, focusing all her attention on the object in front of her.

Summoning all her energy, she felt an irresistible pull toward the cask. She stepped closer and closer, then opened her eyes. She was staring straight at a copper rivet.

Going on gut instinct, she pressed the rivet.

A satisfying click echoed through the basement as the cask swung out from the wall.

"Well, I'll be ... I never knew *this* was here."

Of course, she'd heard the rumors that Isaiah had buried a priceless treasure in a maze under the house, but she didn't think they were actually true. She'd looked before but never been able to find the entrance. In fact, she'd never even paid any attention to the cask.

Her mother and brother must have emptied the basement out at some point. Which made her wonder who else know about the secret maze.

Did her nieces know about this?

She peered into the dark tunnel. A cold breeze touched her face and she breathed in the briny smell of salt water. If the rumors were true, the tunnel would lead to underground passages that housed the treasure. She remembered something about part of the maze being underwater, but it was worth checking out—the item she'd been searching for could be in there.

She slipped into the dark tunnel, a smile playing over her lips as she picked her way along the dark, damp passage.

***

Guilt tugged at Jolene's gut as she drove toward the junior college. It wasn't as if she was lying to her sisters—she was simply taking a little detour before going home. No one would be back at the house until after supper so she had a few hours before anyone even knew she wasn't there.

That should be plenty of time to see if her hunch was right, and return safely home.

Swinging her car into the large parking lot, she drove toward the building, her heart lifting when she saw Gail's Subaru. Hopefully she'd get the proof she needed and put this case to rest today.

She parked far away from Gail and, just in case she was wrong, grabbed her camera and headed into the building.

Jolene's footsteps echoed on the shiny tile of the empty halls. It was almost suppertime, so the daytime classes were over and most of the evening ones had not yet started.

She navigated the halls, peering into the rooms through the rectangular glass windows. The place was like a tomb, which normally would have had her tuning up her senses so she could be aware, but right now she was too focused on her hunch to think of anything else.

She turned down a hall, her nose wrinkling at the smell. Something was burning—she must be on the right track.

A few doors down, she saw it. Flattening herself against the wall, she peeked unobtrusively into the room.

It was just as she suspected. Gail stood just inside the room, a handsome professor to the right of her next to the stove where a pot was releasing steam into the air. Gail wore a white apron and several other students stood beside her.

Gail wasn't having an affair—she was taking cooking lessons!

Just to be sure, Jolene heightened her senses to take a peek at Gail's aura. It was bright blue, not a drop of muddy colors or hint of deception. There wasn't any red or pink either, so Jolene had a pretty good idea that Gail didn't have designs on her handsome teacher.

Angling herself so she could snap some shots without being seen, Jolene put the camera up to her face and got the evidence she needed.

Her task completed, she practically skipped down the hallway. She couldn't wait to tell Steve. Today had been productive—she'd closed a case and discovered something about her mother's death ... well, assuming Barnes being at the bottom of the Atlantic actually had something to do with her mother's death.

She slowed her pace and chewed her bottom lip, deep in thought. What was Barnes jaw doing at the bottom of the ocean? Was the rest of him there? And *who* had put him there and why?

Mae had said the *Andrea June* held the truth and Barnes certainly was keeping some kind of evidence on the boat. Plus he had that photo in his storage locker. Someone must have wanted to stop him.

Maybe the same person who knocked her out and took the photo.

But why wouldn't they have taken the photo and gotten rid of the evidence on the boat sooner? Maybe they hadn't known about them until Jolene started poking around and led them straight to the evidence. Or they figured since Barnes was dead there was no one to blackmail them with the evidence.

Pushing the metal bar on the door open, Jolene walked out into the perfectly sunny summer day. But she didn't feel the warm sun or hear the chirping birds or see the three men in gray hoodies approaching from the woods—she was too deep in her thoughts. Thoughts of Barnes and what he knew about her mother, whose death was now looking less and less like suicide.

When her senses kicked in, it was too late. The men were upon her.

She felt the odd draining feeling similar to the other day and whirled around, pushing out her palms in a thrust of energy.

Her stomach sank. Panic spread through her as she watched the energy dribble uselessly to the ground just before her legs gave out on her.

Everything was happening in slow motion. It seemed like it took several minutes for her to slide down to the ground. Her eyes fluttered, trying to stay open. She watched as the men came toward her, one of them holding out the strange geode she'd seen the other day.

They reached for her and she tried to struggle, to kick out, to fight them off with her hands, but she was too weak.

She felt a pin prick in her neck. Then nothing.

Chapter Eighteen

"Is that the necklace Cal couldn't stop talking about all the way home?" Celeste asked Morgan and Fiona who were bent over the kitchen island studying something.

"Yep." Morgan said without even looking up.

Celeste walked to the opposite side of the island and put her forearms on the cold granite so she could lean over to get a better look at this magical locket. She was disappointed to discover it didn't look like much.

"That's it?" Celeste scrunched up her face. "It's kind of ugly."

"Maybe, but it's pretty special." Fiona slid it toward Celeste. "Touch it."

Celeste gave her sister a funny look, then reached out toward the locket, placing her fingertips gently on top. The tingly sensation was unusual, but not altogether unpleasant. Celeste felt a rush of energy. She pulled her hand back, her cheeks flushed.

"Wow. What was that?"

"We're not sure," Morgan said. "It seems to play off our gifts or something. Cal didn't feel it so I think it only affects people with paranormal abilities."

"I bet it has something to do with the stone," Fiona added. "It's like some kind of an amplifier, but I don't know if all meteorites do it or if this one is special."

"Have either of you ever held a meteorite?" Cal asked.

The three of them shook their heads. "Not that I know of. But I think we should get one and see how it reacts," Morgan said.

Celeste tilted her head to study the design and workmanship of the locket. "It does look pretty old. Did the owner know anything about it?"

"When she dropped it off, she said it was her grandmothers," Fiona said. "When we found out it was more than just a piece of jewelry, we tried to call her but the phone number she gave us was disconnected. We've been asking around town, but no one seems to know her."

Cal's forehead creased. "Where's Jolene? I'm sure she can dig something up about either the owner or the locket."

Morgan waved her hand distractedly. "She's not here. She must have gone out with Eliza or something because her car is gone and neither of them are here."

Celeste's brows knit together. "She's not here? She was supposed to come straight home after she dropped me off and that was hours ago."

Morgan and Fiona looked up. The three sisters' eyes met and a seed of doubt started to take root in Celeste's stomach.

"She might have come home, but her car wasn't here when we got here," Fiona said. "I'm sure she and Eliza just went out shopping or something. It's probably nothing to worry about."

"I guess you're right. We were talking about how we should do more things with Eliza just this morning, so maybe she was acting on that." Celeste glanced around at the counters. "It would have been nice if she had left a note."

"Well, it looks like someone was here, because someone fed Belladonna." Morgan pointed to Belladonna's dish in the middle of the floor. The girls usually kept it in the corner, but the finicky cat always pushed it out into the room little by little as she picked at her food.

"Yeah, I guess you guys are right."

"So, you can't figure out how to open it?" Celeste asked, pointing to the locket.

Fiona shook her head. "We're afraid to try it inside."

A tap at the kitchen door pulled their attention from the locket and they looked up to see Jake Cooper standing outside. Fiona got up, let him in and greeted him with a peck on the lips.

"Hi, everyone," Jake smiled at them, then his smile faltered. "Where's Jolene?"

"Out with Eliza, I guess," Fiona answered.

"What do you mean? She was supposed to stay at home." Jake's jaw hardened, his mouth set in a firm line.

"When have you ever known Jolene to do what she's supposed to do?" Morgan asked.

Jake nodded. "Good point."

"Besides, if she's with Eliza, she's probably safe, right?" Celeste asked hopefully.

"I guess so." Jake looked down at the locket on the island. "What's so interesting?"

"Someone brought this old locket to the shop for me to fix," Fiona explained. "But it seems to be much more than just a piece of jewelry. It seems to be some sort of paranormal power amplifier."

"Huh?" Jake scrunched his face at her. Even though he'd seen the girls 'gifts' in action, he still had a hard time accepting their paranormal abilities.

Fiona simply shrugged. "You'll see."

They went back to studying the locket when they were interrupted again, this time by the front door slamming and the pounding of footsteps running down the hall toward the kitchen.

Celeste tensed, jerking her head toward the door where Luke came practically skidding into the room.

"Sorry, I came as soon as I heard," he said.

Five pairs of eyes narrowed in his direction.

"Heard what?" Morgan asked.

"Don't you know?"

"No. What?" Her voice turned impatient.

"I just got off the phone with Dorian Hall. Jolene's been taken."

***

Taken? Celeste's heart twisted painfully. "What do you mean?"

The room was silent, everyone's attention riveted on Luke.

160

"Dorian had someone following Jolene, but her guy couldn't stop them. They grabbed her at the junior college."

"What was she doing *there*?" Morgan looked at the group. "How did they grab her in broad daylight?"

"That's a good question. Just this morning, she thought someone was following us on a job and she practically set the town on fire with an energy ball. It would be pretty hard to grab her."

"Unless they got her by surprise, or counteracted the energy ..." Fiona looked down at the locket. "If this stone can amplify energy, maybe other stones can absorb it."

Celeste looked around the room. "Wait a minute. If someone grabbed Jolene, then where is Eliza? I thought they were together."

"Maybe she got grabbed too," Morgan answered.

"Or maybe she is one of the 'grabbers'," Cal suggested.

"I'm sorry I don't know much more about it. I feel like we've been kept in the dark," Luke said. "Dorian is coming over to explain."

"Yeah, well, she better." Morgan grabbed the locket. "I think I'll just put this in the drawer. We're not sure we want this Dorian person knowing about it."

"Why not?" Luke looked at her strangely.

"We'll tell you later—"

A knock at the door interrupted them and Luke and Morgan went to see who it was. They returned a few seconds later with a tall, shorthaired woman.

"Everyone, this is my boss, Dorian Hall," Luke went around the room introducing the three sisters, Jake and Cal.

Celeste studied the woman as she shook hands with each of them. Her short hair was stylish but not overly done. She wore black slacks, a black cotton shirt and a gray linen blazer. She would almost be bland—nondescript—but there was something about her that made her stand out—an air of power or authority, which was accentuated by keen intelligence in her large, dark eyes.

"I'm sorry about Jolene. We haven't had time to put enough people in place and there wasn't enough of a force to stop them from grabbing her. We didn't expect her to be out alone." She cocked an eyebrow at Luke.

"She's strong willed," he said.

"Well, anyway, now we know the threat against you girls is very serious."

"What threat?" Morgan demanded. "Who are these people and *where* did they take my sister."

Dorian sighed. "We're not positive, but it seems she's been abducted by people under the control of Dr. Mortimer Bly."

Morgan's brows snapped into an angry 'V'. "Mortimer Bly? Who the hell is that? He sounds like something from a comic book."

"He's one of the world's foremost researchers for alternative energy."

Fiona snorted. "Seriously? What would an alternative energy researcher want with Jolene?"

Dorian and Luke exchanged a glance and Luke gave a half shrug.

"He's not *just* a researcher," Dorian continued. "That's a front for his real purpose."

"Which is?" Cal prompted.

"Tapping into paranormal energy for his personal gain." Dorian nodded toward Morgan, Fiona and Celeste. "Imagine what you could do if you had an army of people with your powers."

Uneasiness bloomed in Celeste's chest. "Do?"

"If you wanted to use your powers to influence others or gain something, you probably could, right?"

"I never actually thought about it." Celeste looked at her sisters who shook their heads. "We've always just used them to defend ourselves."

"Of course, but Bly wants to use those powers —or powers like yours—for more sinister reasons."

"Like what?" Jake asked.

Dorian shrugged. "Money and power, of course."

"Wait," Fiona cut in. "You said powers *like* ours. Do you mean there are others out there like us?"

"Yes," Dorian said. "Although we think your powers are stronger than the others we have seen."

"So what does all this have to do with Jolene?" Morgan asked.

"We think Bly took Jolene as bait. To try to lure the rest of you somewhere. The four of you are a threat to him and he wants to get rid of you."

Celeste felt a chill run up her spine. Had Bly already 'gotten rid of' Jolene?

"Get rid of us?" The look of alarm on Fiona's face echoed Celeste's thoughts. "But why?"

Dorian shrugged. "I guess he feels like you could screw up the works for him."

"But we don't even care about him or what he is doing," Morgan said. "How could we be a threat?"

Dorian shifted on her feet. "He may be under the impression that we've recruited you to help us thwart his efforts."

"Efforts?"

"To collect key paranormal relics that will strengthen his power."

"Relics?" Cal's left brow inched up and he glanced at the drawer Morgan had put the locket into. "What kind of relics?"

"I'm not entirely sure. But the point is, if he's successful his power will grow. With enough of it, he could overthrow entire governments." Dorian's eyes turned deadly serious. "Even ours."

"So that's why you are interested in all this," Morgan said. "And in us."

Dorian gave an apologetic shrug. "We do what we have to do. But, of course, I never *said* I worked for the government ... and you do get paid well for helping."

Celeste thought back to the last job they had done for Luke's mysterious 'company'. It involved ferreting out a centuries-old treasure and they *had* been paid well. Had that had something to do with these relics she was talking about?

"So what's your plan for getting Jolene back?" Morgan asked.

"Well, we need to figure out where he took her and then assemble a team to g—"

"That sounds like it's going to take too long," Jake cut in. "I'll retrace her steps and ask around town. Someone was bound to have seen something."

"Right, and once you get on her trail, we'll just go and get her back. Maybe we can use some of our paranormal skills to help find her," Morgan said, even though she didn't actually know how to use their skills to locate someone.

"Oh no, you girls can't go," Dorian said.

"Can't go?" Fiona scrunched her face at Dorian. "I don't think so."

"No. It's much too dangerous. If we lose the three of you, it could set all our efforts back decades. I'll put my best people on it and I'll let you know what we find." Dorian glanced at a slim silver watch on her wrist. "I better get to it. I'll be in touch. I can show myself out."

She nodded at them, turned on her heel and started toward the hall. Glancing over her shoulder at them, she said, "Stay put until you hear from me. And don't forget, Dr. Bly has deadly intentions towards you."

The six of them stared at each other while they listened to the clicking of the screen door and the sound of Dorian's car starting in the driveway.

Morgan's voice cut into the silence. "Are we really going to stay put like she asked?"

The sisters looked at each other, then at Jake, Luke and Cal.

"No way!"

Chapter Nineteen

"Okay, so how do we figure out *where* Jolene is?" Morgan asked.

"Well, if this was a one of my cases, I'd retrace the person's steps and go to the place they were last seen," Jake answered.

"Which, according to Dorian Hall, was the junior college," Fiona added.

Jake looked at Celeste. "Did she say anything to you about where she was going or why?"

Celeste's stomach sank. She must have been the last one to see Jolene before she was kidnapped. "No. As far as I know, she was coming straight home. I *knew* I should have rescheduled my classes and stayed with her."

Cal slid an arm around Celeste's shoulders. "Don't beat yourself up. Jolene is a grown woman. It was her own decision to go off by herself."

"Yeah, let's not waste time talking about 'what if's'. We need to be proactive," Luke said. "Let's find out about this Dr. Bly and see if we get any clues as to where he might have taken Jolene."

Jake nodded. "And we need to get out to the college before the trail gets cold. Maybe she left us a clue ... some sort of key as to who took her."

Key.

The word niggled something in the back of Celeste's mind.

"Then once we get an idea of what direction to head in, we can come up with a plan on how to get her back." Luke headed toward the East sitting room. "Where's that laptop? I wan—"

"Wait a minute!" Celeste rushed to the drawer where Morgan had put the old locket. She held it up by the chain, watching the light glint off the garnet stone in the middle as the pendant dangled in front of her. "Grandma said something strange to me the other day. She said 'the key is in the locket'. I thought she meant the one Jolene wore that looked like Mom's, but there was nothing in that locket."

"So you're thinking maybe she meant this one?" Fiona asked.

Celeste nodded. She captured the twirling locket in her hand. Immediately, she felt a vibration from the stone. She closed her eyes, concentrating on the energy she was getting from the locket.

She sensed a presence to her right and opened her eyes to see a light blue swirling mist. She watched as it slowly took the form of an old woman. She was bent over with age, but her eyes glowed with youth.

"The locket is protected ... but inside is what you seek." The voice was barely above a whisper and Celeste had to strain to make out the words. Then the apparition was gone. One small droplet of water fell to the floor as Celeste stared at the empty air.

"What is it?" Morgan asked and Celeste realized the others had all been silently watching her.

"A ghost. An old woman. She said what we seek is inside the locket, but it's protected."

"Protected?" Fiona's forehead wrinkled. She reached out for the locket and Celeste handed it over.

"We need to get this thing open, protected or not." Fiona put the locket on the counter, picked up a knife and stuck it into the opening.

Celeste heard a sizzling sound and smelled the arc of electricity. Her hair prickled.

"Ouch!" Fiona jumped back from the locket, shaking her hand.

"I think it's got some kind of energy that's keeping it from being opened," Morgan said.

"Maybe someone who doesn't have paranormal gifts should try it. The locket doesn't seem to affect us regular people the same way." Cal's lopsided grin made Celeste's heart swell and she couldn't help but feel nervous for him as he picked the locket up.

"I'm not even sure it's worth it," Jake said. "What could possibly be inside that would help us find Jolene?"

"I don't know, but if it gives us a clue on where Jolene is, it's worth finding out." Cal gritted his teeth together and pressed on the clasp.

Crack!

The sound was deafening. Celeste covered her ears just as a light blue beam of energy shot across the room, shattering a ceramic mug into a million pieces, which flew up almost to the ceiling, then rained down on the tile floor in a clatter of shards.

"Damn it!" Morgan ran her fingers through her hair. "We need to find a way to open this! I have a feeling what we need to know is inside."

They were hunched over the island, staring at the locket which was sitting in the center where Cal had dropped it, each of them trying to figure out how to get it open when a cold draft pulled their attention away.

Celeste looked up, her heart jerking when she saw a figure silhouetted in the open doorway leading to the basement.

"I can open it."

***

Fiona's narrowed-eyed glare made Eliza's stomach twist.

"You were down in the basement all this time?" It sounded more like an accusation than a question.

Eliza glanced behind her. "I guess you could say that ..."

Eliza saw the sisters exchange an uneasy glance and she knew they were wondering what she'd been doing down there. There wasn't much to look at. She'd probably have to tell them she'd discovered the tunnels ... too bad she hadn't found the amulet, but she'd get them to help her with that in due time.

Right now, she could tell they needed her help. It was all coming to a head just as she'd been told and she'd have to come clean with her nieces and hope they trusted her if she wanted her mission to end in success.

"That locket is protected with an energy seal. You won't be able to open it yourselves."

"What the heck is an energy seal?" Morgan scrunched up her face.

"It's a paranormal device. People with certain skills can seal anything that has hinges with an energy cypher. Only people skilled in breaking that cypher can open it. It's kind of like picking a lock."

Fiona raised her right brow at her aunt. "And you know how to break the cypher?"

Eliza nodded. "But first, tell me what happened. I know something is wrong and I think I can help."

The girls hesitated. Eliza was afraid they wouldn't trust her enough to let her in, but after a few seconds, Celeste said:

"Oh, what the heck. She knows about the locket and the energy lock. Maybe she *can* help."

"Okay." Morgan nodded and told Eliza how Dorian Hall had told them Jolene had been taken and how the mysterious old woman had brought the locket to their shop earlier that day.

Eliza stared down at the locket on the counter. "This is made from meteorite."

"Do you know something about the locket?" Fiona asked. "Near as we can tell, it seems to have unusual properties."

Eliza glanced up at Fiona. "The stone conducts energy like some metals conduct heat. The meteorite this stone came from has a high concentration of iron and nickel which makes it highly conductive to paranormal energy."

"Is that why I feel all tingly when I touch it?" Celeste asked.

Eliza nodded as she bent closer to inspect the locket. "Yes, it enhances paranormal abilities. All meteorites do, so jewelry made from it would be especially valuable for us para's because wearing it would guarantee that you'd always have something that could amplify your special gifts."

"You've seen jewelry like this before?"

"Not the locket per se ... but I've seen pendants. This is very old. It was most likely owned by an Energy Master."

"Energy Master?" Morgan stared at the locket.

"Someone highly skilled in the art of bending energy—making it do what you want. You know what I'm talking about, right?" Eliza's ice-blue eyes stared at each of her nieces in turn.

She sensed that in that one look she was making a connection ... a bond that couldn't be broken, stronger even than their bond of family. She just hoped it wasn't too late.

The girls glanced at each other again. Then Morgan spoke for them.

"We know exactly what you mean."

Eliza nodded. "I know you girls have paranormal gifts, just as I do. It's a Blackmoore family trait like the blue eyes. Which is why we have to get Jolene back. It's critical to our cause."

"Your cause?" Jake looked skeptically at Eliza.

"*Our* cause," she replied. "This isn't just about the Blackmore family or even the paranormal community. What Dr. Bly intends to do could spell disaster for the entire human race."

***

Morgan felt a dark sense of foreboding take hold in the pit of her stomach as she listened to her aunt. She'd learned to trust her gut instincts and right now they told her that her aunt wasn't exaggerating about what might happen if Bly's plan came to fruition.

She shivered thinking what might happen if Bly was successful ... and what he might be doing to Jolene right this very minute.

Luke, Jake and Cal, however, were a bit more skeptical.

"So, you expect us to believe this Dr. Bly is some sort of mad scientists whose goal is to take over the world?" Jake's brows had risen almost to his hairline.

"I guess it does sound a bit far-fetched when you put it that way, but basically that's what it is." Eliza shrugged. "He really does have a multibillion dollar company that researches alternative energy, but that's just a cover for his real work."

"Which is?" Luke asked.

"Trying to harness paranormal energy."

"Why would he want to do that?"

Eliza sighed. "You guys probably haven't thought about it this way, but having gifts like the girls have could make one very powerful. Thus far, you've only used your gifts to defend ... but think about what you could do with them if you wanted to use them on the offensive for evil purposes. Those gifts would enable you to control whatever you want. Money. People. Even whole governments. And Bly wants it all."

Jake scoffed. "Surely he couldn't take over a whole government. No one would let that happen."

"No?" Eliza's blue eyes turned hard. "He has a great front with his business and he acts every bit the philanthropist by donating money and helping in the community. For all outward appearances, he's a pillar of society. It works to his advantage because he can do all kinds of experiments in the name of his alternative energy company and no one suspects him. Quite the opposite, really—they think he is helping us find clean energy. He's made a lot of friends, many of whom are politicians. And if he gets enough of them in his pocket, he can control most of the world without anyone ever knowing."

Luke snorted. "I don't think too many world leaders would fall for that."

"Believe me—Bly can be very persuasive ... especially if he is using paranormal powers to do the persuading."

"You mean he has gifts, too?" Fiona asked.

Eliza nodded. "And an army of minions to do his bidding. But, from what we know, his people are not as powerful as he needs them to be and we fear he is experimenting with ways to boost their power."

Morgan's eyes slid over to the locket. "You mean with rocks and crystals that amplify paranormal abilities like meteorites?"

"That's part of it. The other part is the ancient relics—items infused with amplifying powers by the old Energy Masters. The more of these he has in his possession, the more his powers grow."

"So, there are others with gifts like ours?" Celeste asked.

"Yes, and they use them for both good and bad purposes," Eliza said. "Unfortunately, Bly has recruited a lot of people with gifts to his side —the lure of riches and power is too compelling for most."

Cal leaned against the counter, arms crossed on his chest. "If there are so many people with gifts, why have we never heard of them? You'd think they'd be everywhere, shooting out energy bolts when they get mad or want something."

"There are quite a few with these abilities, although not everyone can shoot out bolts of energy. The abilities manifest themselves differently in everyone. But, as you may have already figured out, it doesn't pay to advertise that you have paranormal gifts so mostly we keep quiet about it."

"I still don't understand why he took Jolene." Morgan asked.

"You girls are very powerful ... more than most. My guess is you haven't even realized the extent of your abilities yet."

Morgan pressed her lips together. It was true, she hadn't spent much time honing her skills, but she could feel them growing stronger every day.

Celeste spoke up from the other side of the room, her forehead etched in a frown. "Wait a minute ... do you think Bly had something to do with our mother's death?"

Eliza's eyes took on a faraway, glassy look. "It's possible. Your Mom was very powerful, too, so you girls have paranormal gifts from the Blackmoore side and her side. We're not sure what happened to her, but I'm certain Bly would have either wanted to turn her to his side or get her out of the way."

"So Jolene was right," Celeste said.

Morgan frowned at Celeste. "Right about what?"

"She had a hunch that Mom didn't jump off that cliff. She was investigating it and had come up with some compelling evidence, too."

"Like what?"

"Well, for one, their one witness, Earl Whiting, seems to have acquired some items beyond his price range. Mae told her the truth was on a boat in Perkins Cove."

Jake narrowed his eyes at Celeste. "You mean the *Andrea June*?"

Celeste nodded.

Jake snapped his fingers. "I *knew* you guys had something to do with that boat blowing up!"

"I always had a feeling Mom didn't kill herself ... but how does this help us find Jolene?" Fiona asked.

"I'm not sure it does," Celeste said.

"Right, then we can revisit it later, but now we need to get to Jolene before she gets hurt ... or worse." Morgan slid the locket over to Eliza. "Open it."

Eliza eyed the locket suspiciously. "Are you sure? What makes you think it will help us find Jolene? It could have been planted by Bly and there could be anything in here ... once I open it, we may not be able to stop it."

"You think it could be a trick?" Fiona looked uncertainly at Morgan. "You have to admit it's kind of strange that the woman who brought it seems to have mysteriously disappeared."

"No. It's not a trick," Morgan felt sure of it. "I can feel it. Plus Celeste said that grandma *told* her the key was in the locket."

"My mother would know. She wouldn't steer you wrong." Eliza picked the locket up in her hand and closed her eyes.

Morgan watched in fascination as pink energy swirled out of Eliza's hand and encased the locket. The energy swirled tighter and tighter until it looked like it was strangling the locket. The locket bulged impossibly, and then a blue mist puffed out of it turning into tiny particles that floated through the air like dandelion seeds before disappearing in a poof of white.

Eliza dropped the locket on the counter and staggered into a chair.

Morgan rushed to her side. "Are you okay?"

Eliza's lips curled in a wan smile. "I'm fine. It's just such an energy drain to unlock a cypher. I believe I was successful, though. Why don't you see if you can open the locket."

Morgan's stomach twisted as she looked at the locket sitting innocently on the counter. What if she was wrong and it was a trick sent by Dr. Bly to harm them?

She reached out, her fingers curling tentatively around the locket.

"Go on," Eliza prompted.

The room fell silent and Morgan put her thumb on the clasp.

She pushed.

Click.

The locket flipped open.

Chapter Twenty

Morgan jumped back as a beam of bright white light spread out from the locket, projecting itself into the middle of the room. She watched, fascinated, as the projection formed into a 3-D image of a rocky island.

"It's a hologram," Cal whispered.

Fiona walked toward it, waving her hand in the middle of the projection, then turned to face the rest of them. "But what *is* it?"

Morgan shrugged. "Looks like an island."

"It's Fury Rock." Eliza stared at the hologram that was still forming. "Bly has a research facility there now. It's at the very top, although it's not part of this hologram."

Morgan frowned at the top of the hologram. The surface of the island was flat and looked large enough to house a compound of buildings. But the hologram showed much more than that. The high cliffs that rose out of the ocean contained several caves and what appeared to be a map of those caves seemed to be forming in the image. "What's all that in the cliffs?"

"A tunnel system." Luke walked around the hologram, looking at it from all angles.

"That's where they're keeping Jolene," Eliza said. "That's why my mother said the key was in the locket. It's a map of the tunnels."

"We can use the map to break her out!" Fiona pulled open a drawer, took out a pad of paper and a pen and started to quickly sketch the map of the tunnels.

"Good idea." Jake started toward the east parlor. "I'll get the laptop and we can figure out where this island is and how to get there."

"It's in the Caribbean," Eliza said. "But it's going to be tricky. As you can see, there's not much around to camouflage your approach. I'm sure Bly has staff disguised as security guards that are monitoring the entrances and exits of the building as well as looking for approaching vessels."

"I'm sure he's expecting us. That's why he took Jolene, right?" Luke rasped his hand across the stubble that was forming on his chin. "So, he'll be on alert—waiting for our arrival."

"Then we'll sneak in at night," Celeste said.

Morgan turned to Eliza. "He won't know we have this map, will he?"

Eliza chewed her bottom lip. "I don't think so. There's no way for him to know this map—or the locket for that matter—even exists."

"Then we have an advantage." Jake slid the laptop onto the counter and started tapping on the keys. "He'll expect us to land on the island on the beach side, but since we have a map of the caves, we can surprise him with an approach from the cliff side."

"Excellent. Let's go." Celeste started for the hall.

Luke held up his hand. "Wait a minute. We need to plan this out properly and make sure we have the right equipment and people. I know you're in a hurry to get to Jolene, but if we don't do this right we may all end up captured by Bly and that won't help Jolene at all."

"Luke's right, but that's not all we need to do." The tone in Eliza's voice caused everyone to stop what they were doing and look up at her.

"What do you mean?" Morgan asked.

"We need to find something to bring with us. Something that I'm sure is in this house. Something that could mean the difference between life and death for all of us."

***

So, Eliza had *been searching the house for something*, Celeste thought, remembering how Jolene had found her in the attic and how they'd seen her come up from the basement the twice now.

"What could possibly be in the house that would mean the difference between life and death?" Cal asked.

"An obsidian amulet," Eliza replied.

"Is that why you were in the basement?" Morgan nodded toward the basement door.

"And searching the attic the other day," Celeste added.

Eliza nodded. "I know they are both filled with old family stuff. Heirlooms. I searched the areas where the older items are in the attic, but didn't have any luck. I remembered that there were rumors about a maze of tunnels under the house with a supposed buried treasure. The basement was loaded full when I lived here so I never really explored down there, and since I couldn't find the amulet in the attic ..."

"But you didn't find any treasure," Morgan said.

Eliza shook her head. "Nope, just a bunch of damp, dark tunnels. I almost got lost down there."

Celeste glanced at her sisters. There *was* a treasure down there ... just not one that you could get to right now.

"We'll fill you in on that later. Right now we should try to figure out where the amulet could be." Celeste hoped it wasn't in the treasure under the house since no one would be able to access it for another three hundred years—at least not without specialized equipment.

"I still don't get why this amulet is so important." Jake's green eyes were loaded with skepticism as they peered over the laptop screen at Eliza.

"Obsidian absorbs paranormal energy, but this one is special."

"Special? How?" Fiona tilted her head.

Celeste was wondering the same thing. She wasn't as well versed in crystals as Fiona, but she did know obsidian could absorb energy ... she just couldn't imagine how that would help save them from death.

"It belonged to Mariah Blackmoore. She had very powerful paranormal abilities," Eliza said.

"You mean our great-great-great-great-great-great grandmother? ... or did I miss a few 'greats'? Fiona asked.

"Yes, Isaiah's wife. She wasn't from here. He met her in his travels in the Caribbean and she was very powerful. It's her power that is handed down through the generations to us," Eliza replied.

"And the blue eyes?" Morgan asked.

"That, too. Anyway, they fell in love and he brought her here. Built this house for her ... well, the original parts anyway. " Eliza looked around the newly remodeled kitchen. "Mariah was a healer and had a way with crystals much like you, Fiona. She imbued the obsidian amulet with an energy infusion which makes it much more powerful."

"Okay, but why do *we* need it so bad?" Celeste asked.

"Bly has an army of paranormals that will try to push bad energy at you. The amulet will help protect the wearer by absorbing the bad energy, rendering it harmless."

"There's just one amulet?" Morgan looked around the group. "What do the rest of us do?"

Eliza shrugged. "Yeah, unfortunately Mariah only infused one. So whoever wears it will have to take the lead in absorbing any negative energy."

"So regular obsidian won't help at all?" Morgan asked.

Eliza shook her head. "In its natural state, it won't be able to absorb enough of the energy. It needs to have its power boosted in order to be effective for our needs."

"We should split up and look for it," Celeste suggested. "We'll be able to cover more ground and hopefully find it faster."

"Good idea." Cal turned to Eliza. "Can you describe what we're looking for?"

"I don't think that's necessary," Fiona cut in. "We won't need to split up. I think I know exactly where the amulet is."

***

Fiona started toward the stairs with Celeste, Morgan and Eliza close behind.

"I searched the attic pretty well and couldn't find it," Eliza said.

"That's because it's not in the attic anymore," Fiona shot over her shoulder as they spilled out onto the second floor.

"You already found it?" Eliza asked as they followed Fiona down the hall to her room.

"We didn't know there was a special amulet in there, but we found an old sack filled with crystals when we were up in the attic a couple of summers ago." Fiona referred to a trip they'd made up to the attic in search of clues to the treasure Isaiah Blackmoore had buried. "I bet it's in there."

They'd come across the crystals among some of the older items. Fiona had fallen in love with the old stones and rescued them from the attic. It turned out to be a good thing she had, since a couple of those stones helped save them.

Maybe this amulet would prove to be just as helpful, Fiona thought as she reached into the top shelf of her closet and pulled out an old, worn burlap bag, which she placed carefully on the bed.

Eliza sucked in a breath. "The initials, MB ... those are Mariah's."

"We thought so," Morgan said as Fiona carefully opened the flaps on the bag to reveal a selection of crystals in various shapes, sizes and colors.

Eliza pointed to a small, black oblong stone with a crude silver ring at the top. "That's it!"

Fiona reached out and picked it up. "I wonder if all these stones are boosted to be more powerful."

"Why do you say that?" Eliza tilted her head to look at the array of stones.

"A couple of them seemed to exhibit extraordinary behavior," Fiona said.

"You mean that white one that showed us the way in the tunnels?" Celeste pointed to a large moonstone.

Fiona nodded, remembering how the moonstone had lit the way and helped them navigate the tunnels under the house.

"Mariah might have infused all these stones," Eliza said. "That would make sense. But I was only told about the obsidian pendant. That's the one that will help us now."

Morgan reached out for the pendant and Fiona handed it over. She held it up in front of her eyes, then looked at the other girls. "So who is going to be the lucky one that gets to wear it?"

"The wearer of the pendant will have an important and dangerous job. They will have to take the lead and make sure they intercept the negative energy for all of us. One wrong move could mean certain death." Eliza's mouth tightened into a grim line. "I'll wear it."

"Wait. Shouldn't we draw straws or something?" Celeste asked. "It doesn't seem right that you wear it. It should be one of us ... Jolene's sisters."

Eliza shook her head. "I can't risk anything happening to one of you. I came to protect you."

"Protect us?" Morgan's brows scrunched together. "You mean you knew all of this was happening?"

"Yes. That's why I came."

Celeste narrowed her eyes at Eliza. "Why didn't you say something sooner? You could have warned Jolene—maybe she would have been more careful and she'd be her with us now!"

Eliza face flushed. "I wish I had. But no one knew exactly what would happen, just that you girls were in danger. I was told to just quietly look for the pendant and be on alert."

"So some secret society of paranormals sent you to save us?" Morgan crossed her arms over her chest. "I find that hard to believe."

"It does sound kind of crazy, but it's true. You girls have been sheltered from it while your gifts mature, but there are others out there like us. Both good and bad. But you girls ... your gifts are extraordinary. That's why Bly is after you."

Fiona, Morgan and Celeste looked at each other. "What do you mean?"

Eliza pointed to the monogram on the sack. "Mariah's people come from a small island. Paranormal gifts have run strong in her family since ancient times. When Isaiah Blackmoore landed on that island three hundred years ago, they fell in love. She came back here with him and they built the original house here."

"We know all that," Celeste said impatiently. "Well, except for the ancient paranormal gifts part, I guess."

Eliza nodded at Celeste, then continued. "Mariah's people came from the south side of the island. On the north side was another clan whose paranormal gifts were just as powerful. The two clans were always at war and eventually they killed each other off. It was said that any offspring of the two clans would have extraordinary gifts."

"But Mariah married Isaiah and he wasn't from the island," Morgan said.

"That's right. He didn't have paranormal powers. But Mariah's powers have been passed down through the family to your father and to me and to you girls. Mariah was one of the few people who ventured from the island."

"Okay, so why are our gifts extraordinary, then?" Morgan asked. "If Mariah didn't marry someone from the island then wouldn't our gifts be the same as anyone else's?"

"*Mariah* didn't marry someone from the island, but someone else did make it off that island three hundred years ago. From the *North* side," Eliza said. "*That* person was an ancestor of your mother's. She had strong paranormal powers, too. And that means that you girls are children of descendants of the two different clans."

The girls fell silent as they digested what Eliza had just told them. Fiona's thoughts whirled in her head, but one stuck out above the others. "My mother had paranormal abilities?"

"Yes. Very strong abilities." Eliza waved her hand. "Oh, I know she didn't show them to you girls, mostly because you weren't old enough. Only Morgan had begun to show an awareness of it while I was still here ... but mostly she was afraid."

"Afraid of what?" Morgan asked.

"That you'd start to develop them, then someone would find out how strong your gifts were and try to harm you."

"Looks like she was right to be afraid," Celeste said.

"So, she really didn't jump from the cliff. Someone killed her because of her abilities." Fiona felt a chill creep up her spine as she voiced her thoughts.

Eliza looked out the window. "That's what we think. We don't know for sure. But that was one of the reasons I left all those years ago ... so Johanna and you girls would be safe."

"How would that make us safe?" Celeste asked.

"My unique skills bring a lot of unwanted attention," Eliza said. "We agreed it was best if I went elsewhere so the attention wouldn't fall on you girls. But I never stopped caring about you and watching over you. I secretly kept in touch with Johanna until ..."

Her voice trailed off and Fiona's heart twisted —all this time, they'd thought Eliza had just taken off and didn't care about contacting them, but she'd really been protecting them and watching over them.

"Okay, enough of this reminiscing," Morgan cut in, tapping the large face of the watch on the wide brown leather band she wore on her wrist. "We need to get going if we want to save Jolene."

Right," Celeste agreed. "Let's figure out who is going to wear the obsidian amulet."

Fiona chewed her bottom lip. An idea was forming in her mind. She didn't know if she could pull it off, but it was worth a try. "I think I know a way all of us can wear one."

"You do?" Eliza asked

"Yes, get me some obsidian and the meteorite locket."

***

Two hours later, Luke and Jake had a plan of attack, a boat and the necessary supplies on the way. They'd used the hologram to map out a route through the tunnels to the top of the island where the building now stood. That's where they assumed Jolene would be.

Fiona had used the boosting power of the meteorite locket to infuse obsidian amulets for all of them—even Luke, Jake and Cal, who reluctantly wore theirs at the insistence of Morgan, Fiona and Celeste.

The seven of them stood in the foyer, bags in hand and ready to rush out the door. They'd hired a pilot to fly them to the Caribbean where the boat, gear, and a few of Luke's men were waiting.

Luke's phone chirped and he looked at the display, then rolled his eyes. "Hello, Dorian ... yes, we are going to try to rescue Jolene ... no you can't talk me out of it ... well, if you think you need to fire me, then so be it." He punched at the buttons on the phone.

"She threatened to fire you?" Jake asked.

Luke shrugged. "Yep. Wouldn't be the first time, though. Anyway, some things are more important. Besides, it's the government. Their standard operating procedure is to disavow all knowledge when you do something they don't sanction and the best way to do that is to fire me."

"You don't think she'll try to stop us, do you?" Morgan asked.

"She might put out the order, but I'm pretty sure no one is actually going to obey." Luke winked. "I called in a few favors.

"I guess we can't count on them for any help either then," Cal said.

"Hopefully, we won't need it. We have our secret weapons right here." Luke nodded toward Morgan, Celeste, Fiona and Eliza and Morgan's stomach tightened.

Secret weapons?

Morgan suddenly wished she'd spent more time honing her gifts. She hoped they could handle whatever was about to happen.

Jake opened the front door. "Okay, you guys ready?"

"Meow!" Belladonna stood on the stairs looking at them with wide eyes. Her gaze drifted over the various pieces of luggage, then up at Morgan as if to say 'aren't you forgetting something?'

"Sorry, Belladonna, you can't come. It's going to be too dangerous. Brody is going to come over and feed you while we're gone."

"MEOW!" Belladonna voiced her disapproval loudly, then hissed at them, turned her back and trotted up the stairs.

Morgan wondered if she'd find a hairball on her bed when she came back ... if she came back.

Chapter Twenty-One

Jolene shivered on the cold, stone bench as she looked around the strange, white marble-lined cell she'd been stewing in for several hours.

The room had only one solid steel door with a tiny, rectangular window in the upper-middle. She'd already tested the lock and it wouldn't open. In fact, her energy seemed to be muted in this room. She guessed that was the reason for the marble walls. The stone must somehow absorb or mute her paranormal gifts.

Leaning back on the bench, her thoughts drifted to the college. She'd been so happy to find out that Gail was only taking cooking lessons that she'd let her guard down.

Her stomach clenched as she realized how stupid she'd been. If only she'd listened to Jake and Luke and stayed with Celeste or at least paid more attention to what was going on around her. Some investigator she was, letting herself get captured in broad daylight!

But, she *had* been captured, knocked out by some weird gizmo that zapped the energy from her. She wasn't even sure where she was or how long it had taken them to get her here, since she'd been asleep for some of the time. The only thing she remembered was being dragged down a series of tunnels and shoved unceremoniously into this room.

Luckily, she'd been awake enough to pay attention to the route through the tunnels and that route was engraved in her photographic memory like a map.

Jolene knew there was no sense in kicking herself over the bad judgment that caused her to be captured. Right now she needed to focus on finding a way out. But the only other opening besides the door was a rainbow shaped hole in the marble wall near the floor. It reminded her of a mouse hole but bigger. Not big enough to fit through, though.

Maybe she could use it to break away more pieces of the wall until it was big enough? It was either that, or overpower whoever came for her and make a break for the tunnels.

She was contemplating which plan would work best, when noises at her door made up her mind for her. Looks like overpowering whoever came for her would be quicker.

She curled up on the bench and feigned sleep.

The door clicked open. Jolene focused her concentration on the doorway where she sensed two men. Her nerves tensed as they stepped into the room.

"I think she's asleep," one of them said. The footsteps came closer. They were beside her now —she could feel the waves of vibration from their energy.

Her eyes snapped open and she launched herself off the bench. Her palms pushed out toward the energy, which she now could see was a giant of a man with broad shoulders and a thick neck the size of a tree trunk.

He jumped back and her heart sank as they both watched a stream of pale blue energy dribble out of her hands and pool on the floor before vanishing.

Thick Neck wasn't taking any chances, though, and he produced a large rock with a rainbow colored geode in the center. He aimed it at Jolene and she felt the energy drain out of her just like it had at the storage facility and the junior college.

"Stop that, you idiot! You'll drain all the paranormal essence out of her!"

Jolene whipped her head around at the familiar voice. "Mateo!"

Her mind whirled with confusion. She'd always thought Mateo, her mysterious guardian angel who had shown up and saved her on several occasions, was her friend ... a few times she'd felt he might be even more than a friend.

Had he really been working with an enemy the whole time? Saving her just for this strange encounter?

Mateo grabbed her right elbow and jerked her to her feet, ignoring her questioning look. He indicated for Thick Neck to hold onto her left side, which he did none too gently.

"Let's get her to the lab. Bly is waiting," Mateo barked out the words and she was propelled through the door.

They dragged her down the shiny gray tile hall, her feet barely getting a chance to move on her own. On the way, they passed another steel door with a rectangular window like hers.

Was someone else being held captive in that room?

At the end of the hall, they shoved her into an elevator and pressed a button, which took them up four floors by Jolene's estimation. The doors accordioned open and Jolene spilled out into a cavernous room that looked like some sort of laboratory with shiny stainless steel tables loaded with beakers and test tubes. Jolene inhaled the bitter scent of sulfur, her heart stuttering as she eyed the centerpiece of the room—a bulky, stainless steel chair.

The chair gleamed under the halogen lighting, but what caught Jolene's attention were the wide leather restraints on the arms and legs. The chair was pierced with dozens of holes, each of which had a clear plastic tube running from it. The tubes ran into a large glass container, which sat empty on the floor next to the chair.

What the hell is that thing for? Jolene felt a chill work its way up her spine as she wondered if the chair was meant for her.

Her attention drifted to a man in a nicely tailored charcoal gray business suit standing at the other end of the room with his back to them. In his hand, he held a laboratory flask by its thin neck, the triangular bottom glowing eerily with a red liquid. He lifted it to the light and swirled the liquid around, a pink mist drifted out of the top of the flask, spiraling toward the twenty-foot high ceiling.

Jolene thought this might be a good time to put up a fight, but her arms were clamped down in the vise-like grips of Mateo and Thick Neck. She squirmed around anyway, but her energy was low and her squirms didn't amount to much.

Slowly, the man turned to face them.

Jolene didn't know what she had been expecting. Some sort of maniacal looking monster, she supposed. But this man was ordinary looking. Medium build with brown hair parted on the side. His bangs fell over his forehead partially obscuring one of his beady black eyes.

He came toward her, staring at her with a predatory look that made her very uncomfortable.

"Ahhh, Jolene Blackmoore. It's such a pleasure to finally meet you." His voice was harsh and raspy. He nodded at Mateo and Thick Neck. "Release her."

They let go and she fell to the ground, cursing herself for not being able to stand on her own. She hadn't even realized the two men were holding her up. She made a mental note to find out what the heck was in those geodes and avoid them if at all possible in the future.

Struggling to her hands and knees, she looked up through the brown curls falling in her face. "Who the hell are you?"

The man laughed. "Why, I'm Mortimer Bly. Dr. Bly, the scientist. Perhaps you've heard of me?"

"No." Jolene rocked back on her feet, trying to stand. Mateo reached out instinctively to help her, but she batted his hand away. She didn't need help from traitors like him.

Bly sighed. "Well, perhaps it's just as well. I doubt we can become friends."

He turned to Thick Neck. "Put her in the chair."

In an instant, Thick Neck's hand wrapped around her upper arm, crushing it and almost bringing her back down to her knees. She tried to pull away, her heart fluttering frantically in her chest as he dragged her toward the chair.

He pushed her down into the chair and she stilled, trying to focus all her energy. But it was no use, she was too panicked. She tried pushing out some energy but only succeeded in exploding a glass tube on the other side of the room. White goo melted out of the tube in a puddle on the counter, then dripped thickly onto the floor.

"Is that all you can do?" Bly lifted a brow at her. "I see you have some spunk, though. Hopefully I will be able to use some of it."

Jolene didn't answer. She was too busy wondering what he meant about using some of her spunk. She didn't like any of the answers that popped into her head. Thick Neck got busy securing the leather straps on her arms and legs, making sure to pull them tight enough so they bit painfully into her flesh.

Panic lapped at her stomach as she looked around at the tubes and flasks. "What is this thing? What are you going to do to me?"

"I'm going to do what I do best, of course. I'm famous for my research on alternative energy. Except this research isn't about energy for powering homes, running manufacturing plants or fueling cars. No ... this is for powering an army. An army of paranormal troops." He tapped the red beaker of liquid. "And this is the key."

Jolene frowned at the beaker. "What *is* that?"

A gleam lit Bly's eye. He put the beaker down, staring at it lovingly for a few seconds.

"It's paranormal essence. I've devised a method of extracting paranormal abilities and distilling them into a liquid that can enhance the powers in others. Even the lowliest skilled para can increase their powers ten-fold with this drink. If only I could figure out how to make it synthetically ..." His voice drifted off as he gazed at the beaker. Then he whirled around to face Jolene. "But I can't. I need to extract if from a human ... and that's where *you* come in."

Jolene shrank back, her eyes darting wildly to the tubes. "You can't!"

Bly's evil chuckle caused Jolene's blood to freeze in her veins. She struggled with the restraints as she watched him flip a series of switches. A low buzz filled the room.

"Oh, but I can. And I have. In fact, you wouldn't believe who I've done this to. It's quite successful, though I do need more testing to make the serum last longer for those who ingest it."

"My sisters will be coming for me. You'll regret this." She twisted and bucked in the chair.

"Oh, I hope they do. I could use their essence, as well." Bly stood before her and leaned in so that his face was very close to hers. The repugnant smell of stale coffee and garlic made her nose wrinkle. He cupped her chin with his hand, his blank, black eyes drilling into hers. "But yours is the best, you're the most powerful. When you're all used up, then I'll tap into them."

Bly straightened and walked over to a big red switch.

Jolene's heart beat against her ribcage. "You can't—"

"Wait!" Mateo yelled, but it was too late.

Bly flipped the switch.

Jolene felt a nerve-shattering jolt of electricity run through her. The air was sucked out of her lungs and her whole body stiffened, almost lifting her out of the chair. Her mouth opened in a silent scream.

As Bly stared at the beaker next to the chair, his leering smile collapsed into a frown. He glanced up at Mateo. "Nothing is coming out."

"Of course not." Mateo strode over to the switch and flipped it off. Jolene collapsed back into the chair, panting. Beads of perspiration dripped from her forehead.

"She's too weak." Mateo thrust his chin out at Thick Neck. "This idiot used the geode on her before we came and they drained her good when they captured her. She needs rest before her powers will be back to full levels."

Bly rubbed his chin, his disappointed eyes darting from Mateo to Jolene to the beaker. "Very well then, take her back to her cell. Give her two hours!"

Bly spun on his heel and turned his attention to the red beaker on the table in the back of the room.

Chapter Twenty-Two

Fury Rock jutted out from the ocean at an impossible height, which, even in the black night, seemed to cast a shadow of foreboding on the small rubber raft that Morgan sat in with Luke, Fiona and Jake.

She steered the raft from the back, glancing behind her to make sure the second raft with Cal, Celeste, Eliza and Luke's main man, Buzz, was following. Satisfied that they were, she turned forward again. It was rough going now that they were so close to the island where the frantic bobbing of the ocean waves made it challenging to navigate between the sharp, jagged rocks that stuck up everywhere.

In the front of the boat, Luke gave the signal to move inland and she expertly maneuvered the boat to a cave-like opening up ahead. She didn't need Luke to guide her, her gifts were on high alert and she knew exactly where to put in.

Securing the rafts was no easy task. There was no beach here, just the steep incline of the cliff and the sharp rocks leading from the cliff into the ocean. Somehow, Morgan managed to find a rock where she could wedge the metal trident into a crevice to hold the boat in place. They'd need it later to get away.

Buzz found a place to tie up the second boat and the eight of them carefully picked their way over the slippery rocks and into the cave. Morgan glanced back at the boats—she hoped Jolene would be able to make her way out to them for their escape ... *if* the rafts were even still there.

The inside of the cave smelled like rotting seaweed. Morgan had to breathe through her mouth until she got used to the smell. Luke had supplied them with night vision goggles and Morgan noticed that even though the walls were weathered with age, the manmade chisel marks were still evident. Someone had carved out this series of tunnels centuries ago.

A rustling sound pulled her attention back to the group, where Luke was unfolding the map they'd drawn from the hologram. They'd brought the meteorite locket with them, too, but looking at the map on paper was easier than trying to navigate with the hologram.

"It looks like we should take this tunnel to the right, then follow that until it branches to the left." Luke said.

"Sounds like a plan." Jake started off to the right.

Morgan clutched the obsidian amulet hanging around her neck for good luck and followed the rest of them into the dark tunnel.

***

The hard, unemotional look on Mateo's face twisted Jolene's gut as he undid the leather straps that held her to the chair. When he was done, he jerked her up by her elbow and Thick

Neck came in to help with the other side. She was too weak to get up on her own.

Jolene remained silent as they dragged her out of the room and into the elevator—she was trying to store up her strength for her next attack. She'd need to have her full powers about her the next time she tried to escape. It might be her last chance.

Once the elevator doors opened, she could walk on her own. The two thugs kept their hands on her arms to discourage any attempts at escape.

Halfway down the hall, she spotted the other door. She'd forgotten about it while she was strapped to the chair, but now felt overwhelmingly curious as to who was inside. Probably some poor sap like her who was getting her energy drained by Bly.

If there were some way to communicate with them, she might be able to form an alliance that could help her escape.

As they passed the door, she pretended to falter. She fell against the door, using the opportunity to peek in through the window.

Her heart skidded. An old woman sat bent over in a wheelchair, her head hanging almost down to her chest. Her long white hair covered her face. Her withered hands clutched at the armrests.

She'd only looked in for a split second before rough hands pulled her away, but Jolene couldn't help but wonder if that was what would happen to her after a few of Bly's sessions in the chair.

They pushed her into her cell and she stumbled over to the stone bench. She was still weak, but could feel her power coming back minute by minute.

"Let's get her locked in here before she regains her strength." Thick Neck stood at the door.

"I'll just make sure she gets what's coming to her after all the trouble she's caused." Mateo advanced on her. Jolene felt a ripple of fear run through her, but looked him steadily in the eye. She wasn't about to let him know how terrified she was.

She opened her mouth to tell him just what she thought of him, but the strange look in his eye made her hesitate.

He pushed her onto the bench, and she cried out, too surprised to speak. In her weakened state, she was no match for him.

She fought not to shrink back when he reached out toward her. Let him do what he wanted—she would not show fear.

His fist curled around the locket and she felt the sting of the chain biting into her skin as he ripped it from her neck.

"That will teach you to resist." He kicked out at her, missing and kicking the bench instead. Then, in two long strides, he was through the door and slamming it shut without even a backward glance.

Jolene rubbed the back of her neck to ease the burn where the chain had bit her flesh. Slumping back onto the bench, she tried to calm her thoughts.

What exactly was going on in here?

Apparently, Bly was hooking people up to his fancy chair and draining their paranormal abilities, then making some kind of serum to give to his minions. Jolene wondered how many people he had, and if the condition of the lady in the wheelchair was what happened once they were used up ... and how long it took for that to happen.

A shudder wracked her slim body. Her sisters would be coming for her soon and they'd fall right into Bly's trap. She had to stop that from happening.

But how?

With a sigh, she settled back onto the bench to come up with a plan of escape.

Chapter Twenty-Three

Morgan's intuitive powers had kicked into high gear so she took the lead. They'd been walking for what seemed like an hour, through dozens of twists and turns. The uphill trajectory and slippery surface made it slow going. The night vision goggles gave everything a green tint and Morgan could see a clingy fluorescent moss glowing on the sides of the tunnels. The heavy damp air taxed her already labored breathing and made her want to go slower and slower.

But it wasn't just the air. Her stomach was starting to get an odd feeling, like something was wrong ... and it was growing stronger the further they went.

Morgan slowed her step.

"What's wrong?" Luke stopped directly behind her, putting his hand gently on her shoulder.

"I don't know. I feel kind of funny." Morgan shrugged and took a step forward.

Zap!

A jolt of white-hot pain knocked Morgan backward into Luke who managed to catch her before she hit the ground.

"What the heck?" Morgan squinted at the tunnel in front of her. The view was distorted—like old wavy glass. It shimmered for a second, then went back to normal.

Morgan blinked. "Did you see that?"

"I'm not sure." Luke's concerned gray eyes looked her over. "Are you okay? What happened?"

"It felt like I got electrocuted." Morgan took a tentative step forward.

"Wait!" Eliza pulled her back. "I think I know what it is."

She picked up a pebble and tossed it into the tunnel, but instead of falling a few feet in front of them, it stopped in mid-air. It made a sound like a mosquito hitting a bug zapper. Sparks arced out from the sides of the pebble and then it fell to the ground.

"I was afraid of that." Eliza's tone was grim.

"What?" Cal asked.

"It's an energy shield."

Jake stepped next to the shield and eyed it suspiciously. "That doesn't sound good."

"It's not," Eliza said. "I'm sure this was put in place to prevent people from getting any further into the tunnels. That must mean we're on the right track. The bad news is it also means we are up against someone very powerful."

"Maybe we can get around it," Celeste suggested.

The map rustled as Luke took it out of his pocket and unfolded it. "Maybe there's an alternate route."

"No," Morgan said. "This is the way we should go. It's the way Jolene came."

"How do you know that?" Jake narrowed his eyes at her.

"I just feel it. My instincts are getting stronger and we have to trust them." Morgan grabbed the chain around her neck and pulled out the meteorite locket. "I guess this thing really does amplify paranormal gifts."

"So what do we do?" Cal asked.

Eliza had moved next to the shimmering wall of air. She stood there silently, studying it. "I think I can break it. It's like a cypher. At least I can try."

"Okay." Morgan looked back at the others who all nodded their agreement.

"Let me see the meteorite locket. I can use it to boost my power."

Morgan removed the chain from her neck and handed the locket to Eliza, who wrapped her hand around it and closed her eyes. Everyone was silent, letting Eliza concentrate without being interrupted.

After a few minutes, Eliza reached her hand out toward the shimmering wall of energy. Turning her hand sideways, she sliced into the energy shield. Purple sparks flew out on either side of her hand.

Morgan could see her aunt's mouth tighten with pain, but she kept slicing into the energy shield, parting it like a curtain. Her hand slid to the bottom then she stepped through, holding her blistering hand in the middle to keep the opening from closing up.

"Hurry, come through." Eliza gestured for them to step through after her.

Morgan went first. Eliza's hand slipped a notch and Morgan could see she was struggling to keep her hold on the energy. She gestured for Fiona to hurry.

Fiona glanced at Jake who nodded, and Fiona stepped carefully through to the other side.

"Women first," Luke said. "Celeste, you go next."

"Hurry!" Eliza's hand was slipping lower, the opening getting smaller. Celeste gave Cal a peck on the lips and shimmied sideways through the narrowing opening.

Eliza cried out and then collapsed to the floor. The energy shield snapped shut with a loud crack leaving Luke, Jake, Cal and Buzz on the other side.

***

Jolene could feel the energy being restored to her body as she sat on the stone bench, wracking her brain for a plan of escape. She'd already tried to use energy to open the lock, but it didn't work. Even if she'd had her lock-picking kit, it wouldn't have helped because the lock was electronic.

She sat up on the bench, leaning forward with her forearms on her thighs. Shaking her head, she tried to get rid of the fuzzy feeling in her brain.

It must be this stone, she thought running her hand over the cold, smooth surface. Some kind of marble or quartz. Somehow it must affect her powers.

It didn't much matter because there was no way out of the room. The little hole in the corner wasn't big enough.

Crossing the room, she looked down at the hole, then glancing out the window in her door to make sure no one was watching, she crouched down and peered in.

The smell of seaweed tickled her nose. This must be a passage—but to where? She could smell the ocean and remembered from her arrival they were on some kind of island.

Was there a tunnel behind the wall that would lead her to freedom?

Maybe she could smash the stone and get out through the tunnel?

She'd memorized the route on her way in, but there was no guarantee the tunnel behind this wall was one of the tunnels that she came in through. Still, it was better than sitting here and waiting for Mateo and Thick Neck to come back for her.

She stood back from the wall, closed her eyes and focused with all her might. Using all the force she could muster, she pushed out with her palms. Red energy sped toward the wall, bounced off then smacked into the wall behind her, bounced off that and hit the side wall.

Jolene ducked to avoid being hit by the stream on its way back around. To her dismay, the energy continued to reverberate around the room, getting weaker and weaker until it finally dissipated into nothing.

Jolene's heart sank. It looked like breaking out wasn't going to work.

Movement over by the hole caught her eye. She stared, open-mouthed as a pair of whiskers poked their way through the hole followed by a pink nose, black furry face and large, ice-blue eyes.

"Meow." The cat trotted over and rubbed the side of her face on Jolene's ankles.

"Well, hi there," Jolene said, happy to have friendly company. She bent down to pet the soft jet-black fur, the anxiety that had been clutching her heart easing just a little as she was rewarded with loud purring. The cat jumped up on the bench next to her and that's when Jolene noticed it had something in its mouth.

"Meow." The cat dropped the object into Jolene's lap and she stared down at it in surprise. It was the locket Mateo had ripped off her neck not even an hour before.

"Where did you get that?" She didn't really expect the cat to answer, but she voiced the question anyway.

The cat simply blinked one ice-blue eye at her, then jumped down from the stone bench and disappeared back through the hole.

Jolene picked the locket up, noticing a clinking sound as she turned it over in her palm.

Something was inside, which was strange, because the locket had been empty when Mateo took it.

She glanced out through the window to make sure the hall was still empty, then opened the locket.

Her heartbeat quickened when she saw what was inside—a tiny glass vile containing two drops of red glowing liquid.

Chapter Twenty-Four

"Eliza!" Morgan rushed to her aunt's side. "Are you okay?"

Eliza sat up, groggy but aware. "I'm okay. I just feel very weak."

On the other side of the energy shield Luke, Jake, Cal and Buzz shuffled around nervously. "Can you open this thing back up and let us through?"

Eliza looked at them warily. The air shimmered in between them like someone had stretched plastic wrap from floor to ceiling. "I'll try."

She stood on wobbly legs, reaching her hand toward the shield. Morgan's heart twisted when she noticed how burned Eliza's hand was and realized how much pain her aunt must be in.

Eliza's hand hit the shield and bounced off in a flurry of sparks, causing her to crumple backward in a groaning heap. Celeste caught her, lowering her gently to the ground.

"I'm sorry. I'm too drained to break the cypher. It might take an hour for me to work back the energy I need." Eliza's voice was thick with regret.

Luke paced back and forth on the other side. "Can anyone else break it?"

"I could try." Celeste stood to approach the energy shield, but Eliza pulled her back.

"No. You need skills and practice. It could kill you otherwise."

Luke whipped out his map. "We can't be separated. You guys will have to stay put until we find a way around."

Morgan felt conflicted, restless. She chewed her bottom lip, trying to decide what to do as she watched Fiona bend down and gently take Eliza's burned hand.

"Give me the meteorite." Fiona indicated Eliza's other hand, which still clutched the locket.

Eliza opened her fist and Fiona took the locket, holding it in her palm and closing her eyes. After a few seconds, she removed the carnelian bracelet she was wearing, clutching it into the fist of her other hand and resumed her meditation.

Morgan gaped at Fiona's hand, which looked like it was being lit from the inside. The carnelian stones inside were glowing, the amber light escaping from the spaces between her fingers.

"Here, hold this where the burn is," Fiona handed the bracelet to Eliza who applied it gingerly to her injured hand.

On the other side of the energy shield, the guys bent over the map, picking out a route.

"We'll go up through here, around and come back. It should lead to the other side here." Cal traced the route with his finger.

"That seems like it would take a long time," Morgan said glancing nervously at her sisters. "I don't think we can wait. Jolene needs us now."

"No. No way. It's too dangerous. We're not letting you girls get hurt." Luke gave her his sternest look, but Morgan's mind was made up ... she just hoped her sisters thought the same thing. If they didn't she was willing to go on her own.

"Sorry, Luke, we don't have any time to waste," Morgan said. "Besides we can take care of ourselves, remember?"

Next to her, Fiona was pulling a wobbly Eliza to her feet.

"You girls go on without me. I'll slow you down," Eliza pleaded.

Morgan held up her hand. "No way. You're family and we don't leave family behind."

The smile on Eliza's face warmed Morgan's heart, but she didn't have time to feel all warm and fuzzy—they had to get going before it was too late to help Jolene.

She looked into Luke's concerned, gray eyes.

"I don't like it, Morgan," he said. "How will you know where to go if *we* have the map?"

"We have the hologram in the locket and I can use my intuition." Morgan's heart ached as she turned away from him. She didn't want to be separated from *him* either, but she knew it could be bad for Jolene if she didn't get going—like *now*!

She turned and started down the tunnel without looking back, afraid she might change her mind if she did.

"Wait! How will we know where to meet?" Luke yelled after her.

"Don't worry, I'll figure it out," Morgan shouted over her shoulder without turning.

Morgan could hear Fiona and Celeste coming up behind her. She half-turned to see them supporting Eliza between them. Eliza looked a little unsteady, but was walking with minimal support. Behind her sisters, Morgan could see the worried looks on the guys' faces as they stared after them. Her stomach tightened and she looked forward again and quickened her pace.

"I think they're going to be mad at us," Fiona, who was also looking behind them, said.

"Well, too bad. We have to find Jolene and if that means we split up then so be it," Morgan replied.

"Of course you're right," Celeste said. "It's just too bad that *they* have the guns and Tasers."

***

Loud voices at the end of the hall pulled Jolene out of a fitful sleep.

Had it been two hours already?

She stared at the vial in her hand.

Should she drink it?

The liquid in the vial looked like the liquid in Bly's beaker ... the elixir that was supposed to enhance paranormal powers. She could sure use some enhancing ... and the cat had reminded her of Belladonna. What did she have to lose?

She downed the bitter liquid in one gulp, grimacing as it burned her throat. She got up quickly and shoved the vial into the hole in the corner, then ran back to the bench and tried to pretend she was just waking up.

No sooner had she lain down than she heard Mateo outside the door. "I'll get her."

Jolene could already feel the power surging through her, but something told her not to tip her hand just yet. She'd gain the advantage if Mateo and Thick Neck thought she was too weak to fight. Much better to let her powers increase while she waited for the perfect moment.

The door clicked open and Mateo came into the room toward her, his eyes darting to her neck.

The locket!

Her hands flew up to hide it. She couldn't believe how stupid she'd been to put it back on. How would she explain it being back on her neck?

His eyes jerked up from the locket and met hers, but instead of anger, she saw something else. Satisfaction? Understanding? She wasn't sure what, and equally unsure of how to interpret the strange feeling deep inside her.

He nodded and then grabbed her arm, yanking her up from the bench, but not as roughly as before.

"Time to go," he said as he pushed her to where Thick Neck was standing just outside the room. He grabbed her other arm and the two of them dragged her down the hall while she focused on pretending like she was too weak to walk.

They passed the dark corridor and she wondered if she should try to break away and make a run for it now or wait. Her instincts told her she should wait until she was in the lab. If she had a chance to incapacitate Bly, then he wouldn't be able to order his minions to follow her ... and the less people following, the better her chances.

She let them shove her into the elevator and they rode it up to the lab.

The elevator doors whooshed open to reveal Bly standing beside the stainless steel chair. He looked at Jolene slumped between Thick Neck and Mateo, his mouth quirking into a malevolent smile.

"I hope you are well rested," he leered.

Jolene wrenched her arm from Mateo's grasp, thinking to hit Bly with a whammy of energy first and then take out Mateo and Thick Neck while they were still trying to figure out what was going on. Except it didn't work. Mateo's grip on her arm tightened and she felt a rush of weakness.

Her knees buckled and, before she knew what had happened, she'd been shoved into the chair and Mateo was strapping her in.

Except, something was different this time ... the straps weren't biting into her skin. In fact, he wasn't even securing them at all.

Jolene stared at her arms in stunned amazement, then her eyes met Mateo's. He mouthed the words 'play along'.

Jolene didn't know whether she should trust him or not. He was one of Bly's minions ... or so it seemed. Yet, he hadn't secured the straps and that surely counted for something. She decided to wait and see what he had in mind. A few more minutes wouldn't hurt and she could feel herself getting stronger with each passing second.

Bly wrung his hands together in anticipation. He ripped his gaze from Jolene and turned to Mateo. "Did you amplify the output sources like you suggested?"

What did he mean by amplify? Jolene frowned at Mateo, an uneasy feeling spreading in her chest.

"Yes, I rigged it so it will pull the maximum amount out of her ... I just hope it doesn't kill her." Mateo glanced at Jolene.

Kill her?

Jolene tensed, ready to leap out of the chair on the attack until she saw Mateo shake his head slightly.

Had he read her mind?

Somehow, she knew the headshake was for her and that it meant for her to wait.

Had she read his mind, too?

She sat back in the chair and waited.

"You'll have to wear this protective shield so you aren't harmed." Mateo handed a clear glass helmet to Bly. Two metal posts with a coiled copper spring between them stuck up from the top.

Jolene almost laughed as Bly put it on—he looked like something from a comic book.

Bly adjusted the chinstraps on the cumbersome helmet, then leered at Jolene.

"Hit it!" he yelled, followed by a high-pitched maniacal giggle that set Jolene's nerves on edge.

Mateo flicked the big red switch. Jolene braced herself, but instead of feeling a painful jolt, she felt nothing.

Bly, on the other hand, stiffened, the color leeching out of his face, his eyes bulging.

"Argghhh." He pointed at Mateo, then fell to the floor clawing at the helmet.

Jolene figured Thick Neck wasn't known for his intelligence since he was just standing there, his face a mask of confusion as his eyes darted from Mateo to Jolene to Bly.

She bolted out of the chair, pushing her hand out at Thick Neck. A purple ball flew out of the palm of her hand and sped toward him, smashing into the center of his forehead. His eyes crossed and he fell like a mastodon that had been hit by a meteor.

"Come on!" Mateo grabbed her by the arm and headed for the elevator.

Chapter Twenty-Five

"I can walk on my own now." Eliza shook off Fiona and Celeste. Morgan noticed her hand was almost fully healed.

"Your hand, it's healed already!"

Eliza lifted her hand up, turning it back and forth in front of her face.

"I guess it is." She handed the carnelian bracelet back to Fiona.

"I've used carnelian to heal before, but I've never had it work this fast. That meteorite locket really does enhance our powers. We'll have to get some more meteorites, if we ever get out of here.

"Speaking of which, we better hurry," Eliza said. "I don't know if that energy shield breach triggered an alarm. They could be coming for us right now."

Morgan felt a twinge. She could sense friendly energy—the energy Jolene left behind when she was taken through the tunnel. Even though it was fading, it told her which direction to go. "I think we need to take this right turn."

They turned to the right, but only made it a few feet down the tunnel when Morgan got another twinge—this one not so friendly. She put her arm out to stop the others.

"Someone's coming."

"I don't hear—"

"Shh... They're up ahead," Morgan whispered. Her eyes darted frantically around the tunnel for a hiding place, her stomach sinking when she didn't find one. Her intuition was getting stronger now. Even though the guards were two hundred feet away, she knew they were there and could even tell how many people were coming. "There are five of them. We're out numbered, but we have no choice but to fight them now."

"Meow."

Morgan whirled toward the noise. A black cat sat in the path, her ice-blue eyes blinking at them. She watched as the cat stood up and walked to the wall, then disappeared.

"Did that cat just disappear?" Celeste asked.

"Looks like it." Morgan walked over to the spot. At first glance, it looked like a solid wall, but on close inspection, she could see that the stone overlapped in one spot. There were actually two walls next to each other with a thin space between. Peering in, she could see the cat sitting inside a tiny hidden niche barely big enough to fit the four of them.

"Come here, quick!" She gestured toward the others who filed over and, one by one, slid into the space behind the wall. The opening was barely big enough for them to squeeze through, but they managed. She just hoped the small opening and overlapping walls would hide them from the guards.

A few seconds later, heavily booted footsteps passed by the opening. The guards were talking in hushed whispers. There was no sign by the tone of their voices or their energy signatures that they even suspected the girls were there.

It was a tight fit in the little niche. Morgan felt like she was suffocating. She stepped back to get some breathing room.

"Plink!"

Morgan's heart skidded—she'd inadvertently scraped a rock loose from the wall and it had fallen onto the floor.

"What was that?" The guard's voice sounded from a few feet down the hall.

"What? I didn't hear anything." A second guard.

"I did. Someone is back there."

Morgan held her breath as the sounds of the guard's boots scraping the tunnel floor came closer. She braced herself, knowing they would soon be discovered and have to fight their way out. Beside her, she could feel Fiona tense.

"Meow."

"Oh." The guard let out a chuckle. "It was just a cat. Get outta here. Go on—scoot!"

"Ha, big bad Roger scared of a cat," the other guards laughed.

Morgan's shoulders sagged with relief, but she remained stock still, afraid to breathe.

She heard static. Walkie-Talkies.

"Base to Team one ... come in." The distorted voice sounded far away.

"Team one here," the guard said.

"I'm getting something on the monitor. A disturbance in sector five. Can you check it out?"

"Roger." The static snapped off. "Let's go."

Their boots scuffled off into the distance. Morgan counted to twenty before jostling her way to the opening so she could peek out. No one was in the tunnel.

"It's clear." She waved the others out. "Come on."

"Boy, am I glad we didn't have to fight them," Celeste said, looking around for the cat. "I don't know if we could have beaten them without Jolene."

Fiona pulled three glowing crystals from her pocket. "Not to worry. I brought some of these crystals. Remember how they helped us fight off bad guys before?"

Morgan smiled, remembering the big fight for the treasure under their house. Somehow the crystals knew just who to target and packed a wallop. But they only had three, and she had a funny feeling they were going to need more than that. None of them really had the fighting power that Jolene did.

"That's good to know," Morgan said. "But I'm worried about the disturbance they talked about."

"It could be the energy shield," Eliza suggested.

"Or Luke, Cal, Jake and Buzz." Morgan's forehead creased with worry. "They could be in trouble and none of them have paranormal skills. We'd better hurry."

***

Jolene and Mateo spilled out of the elevator at full speed. Jolene eyed the dark corridor to the right. Somehow she knew that was the best way out, but something tugged her attention away.

The door with the rectangular window—the other cell.

Jolene rushed toward it. To her surprise, Mateo was right beside her. She would have thought he would have wanted to head straight down the dark hallway.

"We can't leave anyone here." Jolene skidded to a halt in front of the door to the old woman's cell. "How many people does he have locked here?"

"Just the two of you," Mateo said.

Jolene wondered why he was looking at her curiously as he pushed a series of buttons on a panel beside the door.

The door clicked open and Jolene rushed in, her heart pinching for the poor woman slumped in the chair.

The woman turned her face toward them. Her amber eyes looked up at Jolene in confusion, then they widened as they drifted down to her locket and then back up to her face.

Jolene's heart stopped beating. She felt dizzy with confusion. She'd know those amber eyes anywhere.

"Mom?"

***

The old woman's eyes filled with tears. She reached out a wrinkled hand and touched Jolene's cheek.

"Jolene? I thought I'd never see you again."

"You're alive?" Jolene's voice cracked with emotion. She whirled around to look at Mateo. "Is this some kind of trick?"

"It's no trick," her mother's voice said. "I've been held prisoner here for a long time. I tried to spare you—"

"What happened to you?" Jolene stared at her mother in disbelief. Her mother had only been dead—well, missing—for seven years. She should be in her early fifties, but she looked like she was eighty.

How was that possible?

Her mother ignored her question. She looked around the room with fearful eyes. "It isn't safe for you. What are you doing here?"

"Getting you out, hopefully," Mateo cut in. "Sorry, there's no time for a family reunion right now. You guys can catch up later, but for now let's get the hell out."

He grabbed the handles of the wheelchair and hurried into the hall, then down the dark corridor. Stopping about halfway down at an elevator, he pressed his thumb into a small pad on the side. The elevator door slid open.

"Where are we going?" Jolene looked inside the elevator nervously.

"I know a way out." Mateo looked back at her. "You have to trust me."

Jolene looked into the elevator then back out at the hall.

Did she hear someone coming?

"Jolene, get in," her mother said. Mateo had already pushed the wheelchair in and was standing with his hand holding the doors open for Jolene. "You can trust Mateo."

Johanna gave her 'the look'. Childhood memories instantly flashed through her mind. That look meant she should listen to her mother ... or else. A half-smile formed on her lips and she stepped inside.

The elevator whooshed them down several floors and the doors opened to reveal the underground tunnel system.

Mateo wheeled Johanna out of the elevator and Jolene followed. She was just starting to think this was too easy to be true when the heart-stopping sound of an alarm split the air.

Chapter Twenty-Six

The shriek of the alarm sent a jolt of adrenalin coursing through Morgan's veins.

"They must have figured out we breached the energy shield!" Celeste yelled over the din.

Or discovered Luke and the guys, Morgan thought.

"We better kick it into high gear," Fiona shouted. "There's a tunnel off to the right that goes uphill, let's take that."

"Okay." Morgan turned to Eliza. "Are you okay? Do you want us to slow down?"

"Slow down?" Eliza scrunched up her face. "We need to speed things up."

She took off at a trot in the direction Fiona had suggested. Morgan looked at her sisters, shrugged and took off after her.

The tunnel ran straight for two hundred feet, then turned sharply to the left. The alarm was so loud, it was impossible to hear anything else, which is why they almost ran right into the three darkly dressed guards who were just around the corner.

Eliza skidded to a stop just in time, her face mirroring the look of surprise on the guard's faces.

The guards held small guns ... not the kinds that used bullets, Morgan deduced with a quick glance. No, these guns held something much more deadly.

She watched as they raised the guns.

"The amulets!" Morgan yelled as she held the obsidian amulet out in front of her.

A greenish brown light shot out of the guns toward them. Morgan knew it was some sort of energy ... energy she didn't want to come into contact with. She angled the amulet toward the energy stream and the stream of light was absorbed harmlessly into the black rock. She noticed her sisters doing the same, but the guards kept firing.

And then the energy streams dried up ... the guns had run out!

Morgan felt a momentary lift of victory until the guards threw the guns to the side and advanced on them. She realized they'd have to fight their way out.

Morgan took a step backward. If she had Jolene's paranormal abilities, she could just shoot some energy at them, but she didn't. She did, however, have something else—her intuition. And right now her intuition was telling her that the largest guy, the one on the right, had a weak spot in his left knee.

She lunged forward, kicking out with her right leg aimed at that very spot.

"Aghh!" The man crumpled to the ground, holding his knee and rolling around on his back. She'd aimed perfectly.

The screams of the guy distracted the guard in the middle and Celeste moved in with some of her karate moves, giving him a heel kick to the jaw.

The third guy must have had some decent paranormal abilities. Morgan noticed that he could push energy from his fingertips, which he was aiming at Eliza and Fiona. The two of them were successfully fending off the energy onslaught with their amulets, but he was advancing on them.

Morgan noticed that they were slowly being pushed back down the tunnel.

"Fiona! The energy balls!" Morgan ran over in front of Fiona, her amulet thrust out in front of her to absorb the energy stream being directed at her sister. "I'll cover you!"

Fiona pulled the glowing red ball out of her pocket, swung her arm back and then lobbed the energy ball between the two guards who were left standing.

The guards watched, mesmerized, as the ball hovered two feet off the floor. Its glow lit their faces from underneath giving them an eerie look that reminded Morgan of when she used to put the flashlight under her chin to scare her sisters in the dark.

The crystal shattered into a million pieces. Shards of energy flew into all three of the guards and the two that had been standing were knocked to the floor.

Morgan noticed it was disturbingly silent. Sometime during their fight, the alarm had stopped sounding.

Eliza peered down at the guards cautiously. "Are they dead?"

Morgan shrugged. "I don't know."

"Who cares?" Celeste held up her palm for a high-five. "We beat them."

The sweet feeling of victory warmed Morgan's chest as she high-fived her sisters and aunt.

Her momentary happiness was shattered seconds later when she heard footsteps pounding toward them.

"Did you hear that?" Fiona's face was pinched with concern.

Morgan nodded. "Run!"

They jumped over the lifeless guards and fled into the tunnel.

***

The wheels of the chair got stuck on every stone and groove in the tunnel, making it slow going. Even though the alarm had stopped wailing, Jolene still felt jazzed with anxiety—she knew Bly's minions were coming for them and they had to get out fast.

In her mind, she brought up the map of the tunnels she'd memorized on the way in, but she couldn't correlate it with where they were now. She realized they must be in a different section that she hadn't seen yet.

"Do you know where you're going?" she asked Mateo.

"Yes, of course." He rolled his eyes at her. "There's a passage down there and I have jet skis tied up in a partially submerged cave. I stored them there just in case I needed to make a quick getaway. Lucky thing I brought two."

"Jet skis?" Jolene glanced at Johanna.

"Don't worry," Mateo said. "She can ride one. She's not crippled. She's just weakened. I'll strap her on one of them with me."

"I don't get it. Were you planning this all along? How did you know I would be here?"

Mateo turned his velvety brown eyes on her and her stomach flip-flopped. *What was that all about?*

"Actually, I hoped you wouldn't be here. But I've been in place here for over a year now, trying to get Johanna out and the jet skis have been—"

"Oh, crap." Johanna's words caused him to stop and they looked down at her. She was staring straight ahead down the tunnel. Jolene followed her gaze, her blood freezing when she saw four beefy guards about a hundred feet away and closing in on them fast.

Mateo immediately stepped in front of Johanna to protect her. Jolene stepped out next to him.

The men were running toward them now. One of them pulled a long, thin pen out of his pocket. It looked to Jolene like some kind of laser pointer and he was pointing it right at her.

"Look out!" Mateo yelled.

Jolene thrust her hand out at the floor causing it to ripple like a towel in the wind. The four men went flying in the air, then thudded back to the ground. The laser pointer gizmo clattered on the floor and rolled away from him.

Jolene looked at her hand. She'd never been able to do *that* before. Apparently, the red liquid worked pretty well.

Mateo gave Jolene a look of appreciation. "Nice work."

She looked up to thank him, her eyes widening as she saw another guard making a grab for him. It only took Mateo a split-second to read the look on her face. He turned around, punching the guard who fell to his knees, holding the bloody crumpled mess that used to be his nose.

It was a short-lived victory, however. The four guards who had been knocked down by Jolene's whammy were struggling to their feet and two more guards were pounding down the tunnel to join them.

They were severely outnumbered.

Jolene grabbed the handles of the wheelchair and whirled it around. "We'll have to outrun them!"

She started back down the tunnel at full speed, stopping short after a few hundred feet when she heard the sounds of footsteps running toward them. She cocked her head to the side to hear better. There were several people coming.

She looked at Mateo. "Are there any side tunnels here that we can duck down?"

The pinched look on his face gave her the answer before he even answered.

"No."

Jolene's heart hammered in her chest as the running footsteps got closer. Glancing behind her, she could see the other guards advancing.

They were trapped.

Chapter Twenty-Seven

Fiona gasped for breath as they ran up the tunnel. Her body wasn't conditioned for running uphill and it was taking its toll. Glancing behind her, she could see the tunnel was clear. The guards hadn't caught up yet, but they'd be on them soon.

Up ahead, Eliza had stopped just before a sharp turn in the tunnel and was holding out her hand in a signal for them to stop. Fiona gladly complied, bending over and resting her hands on her knees to suck in a breath.

"Someone's up ahead of us!" Eliza whispered.

Panic gnawed at Fiona as she glanced behind them. "And the others will catch up any minute."

"What should we do?" Celeste asked.

Morgan closed her eyes for a second. Fiona assumed she was trying to get in touch with her gut feelings to give them some guidance. She knew that sort of thing took time, but she wished her sister would hurry—time was one thing they did not have.

Morgan opened her eyes and barked out the order. "We'll fight off whoever it is up ahead. Maybe we can overpower them by the time the ones behind us catch up."

"Good idea." Fiona had already taken out one of the red crystals. She hefted it in her hand, feeling the power of the small orb. "Let's whammy them with this right away."

"Okay, but aim well ... we only have one more left."

Fiona nodded. Raising the energy ball in the air, she charged forward, rounding the corner at full speed ... and then skidded to a stop, not believing who she had come face to face with.

"Jolene?"

"Fiona!"

Jolene looked past Fiona at her sisters and aunt. "What are you guys doing here?"

"Trying to rescue *you*. Are you okay? What happened?" Fiona turned to look at her sisters. "Morgan, can you believe this?"

But Morgan wasn't paying attention. She was staring oddly at the white haired woman in the wheelchair. Fiona had barely noticed the woman out of the corner of her eye because she'd been so intent on Jolene. She turned to see what had captured Morgan's attention and her heart crashed.

"Mom?"

Fiona looked wildly from Jolene, to Mateo, to Johanna and then back at her sisters.

"There's no time for questions now! Mateo's urgent voice pulled her back to the present situation and she saw their mistake. The hesitation had allowed the guards to catch up on both sides of them.

They were trapped in the middle with nowhere to go.

Kaboom!

The floor under Fiona's feet rocked unsteadily and she lurched against the wall, flinging her hand out to steady herself. She noticed with relief that the blast had slowed down the guards.

"What was that?" Celeste asked.

"They're blasting the exits closed so we can't get out!" Mateo answered.

Kaboom!

This one was stronger. Rocks showered down from above, hitting some of the guards and even knocking a few out. Fiona looked around to make sure no one on her side was hurt. She tightened her hold on the red crystal—they still had guards advancing from both sides and she'd need to make sure she threw it at precisely the right moment.

Then she noticed a dark area on the wall slightly behind her. She leaned back to inspect it and a blast of cold, salty air smacked her in the face. It was an opening!

"Over here!" She motioned for the others to follow her, her heart soaring—this could be their chance to get away.

She scurried through the opening ... and came to an abrupt stop right in front of the biggest hole in the ground she'd ever seen.

Icy fingers clenched her heart as she peered down into the hole. It must have been five hundred feet deep. A quick look around the room told her it was a dead end. There were no exit tunnels—just the hole. Up above, a large metal circle sat directly above the hole, like some sort of sewer grate. Fiona pulled back fearing the metal piece would open, dumping out gallons of sewer water that would wash them all down into the hole.

"Go back!" Fiona screamed. She turned to backtrack but it was too late. The guards were already at the opening.

The only way out now was to jump five hundred feet to certain death.

***

"We can take these guys! Our power is stronger together!" Jolene held out her fist and the sisters placed their hands on top for a quick second then broke free.

Jolene pointed at one of the guards. An arc of white electricity shot out from her finger toward him, vaporizing him on the spot.

"Looks like someone's been practicing," Morgan said.

"That, and I took some booster juice." Jolene pointed at another guard who somehow managed to avoid the deadly energy stream.

Morgan didn't have time to wonder what her sister meant by 'booster juice' because a guard was climbing through the opening toward them. A quick glance at him and her intuition told her he had a weak jaw.

"Celeste—his jaw!" Morgan pointed and Celeste spun around kicking out her heel, landing it square on the guy's jaw.

Snap!

Morgan felt a split second of smug satisfaction as the guard staggered backward, clutching his jaw. But the satisfaction didn't last long. More guards were coming through the opening toward them.

To her right, her mother sat helplessly in the wheelchair. Morgan could feel her anguish. Mateo stood in front of Johanna like a human shield. He threw his hands up and a wave of red unfurled like someone had pulled the end of an invisible carpet and shook it. Two more guards fell backward and lay still on the floor.

"Hold on!" Fiona yelled. She whipped the red ball into the rest of the crowd of guards, who collapsed like bowling pins as slices of red-hot energy ripped through them.

"Let's go!" Morgan grabbed Eliza and pushed her forward. Celeste, Fiona and Jolene scrambled away from the deadly hole and back into the tunnel.

With her sisters out in the tunnel, Morgan stepped back through the opening into the room to help Mateo get Johanna's wheelchair over the rubble of rocks in the doorway when a voice behind her chilled her blood.

"Not so fast."

She whipped around to see a man in a nicely tailored charcoal suit standing there with nine of the biggest, angriest looking guards she'd ever seen. The guards looked to be wearing some kind of high tech armor in matte black with blue neon lights at the joints and big, clunky guns strapped to their sides.

But that wasn't the worst part.

The worst part was that the guy in the suit was holding Luke in front of him, the point of a shiny steel knife jabbing right into the middle of Luke's throat.

***

"Luke!" Morgan's heart twisted and she started toward him, but Eliza pulled her back.

"Let him go, Bly," Eliza yelled.

Morgan stared at the man. So *this* was Dr. Bly, the man Dorian had told them about. She felt a cold finger dance up her spine at the sinister look in his eyes.

"Oh, you want me to let him go?" Bly mocked her. "Sure, just hand over Jolene and Mateo and we'll call it an even trade ... you can keep the old one, I've used her up."

Morgan paused, trying to buy time. The anger was building inside her and it seemed to be heightening her gifts. She could see the vulnerability in the guards and, if she was smart, she would have capitalized on that, trying to take out a few of them, but the anger she had for Bly was welling up like a tidal wave she couldn't control and she could see his vulnerability was his eyes.

She launched herself toward him, her fingers out like claws, intending to scratch his eyes, but before she even reached him, one of the guards thrust his hand out at her.

246

A beam of energy flew out of his special armor, hitting her square in the chest. The breath rushed out of her lungs and she felt like she was trying to run under water. Everything slowed down as she fell backward, toppling into Celeste, who lurched forward at the guard with a perfectly aimed karate kick that ended in a sickening crunch.

Morgan tried to clear her head from the energy drain. Everything was happening too fast. Jolene and Mateo were fighting off the guards on her right. Eliza was busy trying to disarm the guard near Bly and Celeste and Fiona were ganging up on a guard to her left.

She glanced over at Luke just in time to see him haul back and elbow Bly in the ribs. Bly dropped the knife and Luke broke free, running over to Morgan's side.

"Are you okay?" His eyes were dark with concern.

Morgan nodded. She let him help her up, anxious about wasting any time—by the looks of things her sisters desperately needed their help fighting off the guards.

Luke let out a whistle, which momentarily confused Morgan. When Cal, Jake and Buzz came running down the tunnel, she realized the reason for it—they'd been waiting for his signal all along.

Morgan noticed the three men had their arms raised. She realized they were holding the Taser's they'd brought.

Jake aimed his Taser at one of the guards and pulled the trigger. The wires shot out, hitting the guard in the middle of the chest and bouncing off.

"Aim for the chinks in the armor!" Luke yelled.

Buzz did as told, hitting another guard where the upper arm met the shoulder plate. The guard jerked forward, his armor sparking from all the joints, then collapsed on the floor, wisps of smoke rising from his body.

In a flash, the boys were beside them fighting off the rest of the guards. Morgan noticed they were making headway, but something wasn't right—none of the guards had used their guns.

Morgan could see Bly struggling to his feet. He was holding his side, his face contorted in rage.

"Hit them with the dark energy!" his shrill voice echoed in the tunnel.

The guards reached for the clunky guns.

Morgan's stomach twisted. Dark energy sounded bad and the smug look on Bly's face told her this was his secret weapon—his ace in the hole. She reached for the obsidian amulet and held it out in front of her.

Streams of dark brown energy spewed from the guns. Morgan pushed her amulet toward the stream that was headed for her. This energy seemed to be more powerful than the energy they'd fended off earlier and it was a struggle to keep her amulet in its path.

Beside her, Celeste wasn't as lucky—she hadn't gotten her amulet up in time and the dark energy hit her in the stomach, doubling her over. She slumped to the floor.

"Celeste! Your amulet!" Fiona yelled, gesturing to her own amulet.

Celeste made a weak attempt to use her amulet to protect her from the energy stream still coming at her but was too weak. Morgan raced over, helping Celeste with the amulet, interrupting the stream long enough for Celeste to regain enough strength to be able to hold it on her own.

The guys were still trying to take down the guards by aiming their Tasers at the chinks in their armor, but the guards were focused on aiming the bad energy at Morgan and her sisters. Morgan felt thankful Fiona had made amulets for all of them and then came the gut-wrenching realization that one of them didn't have an amulet.

Jolene.

Morgan glanced over at Jolene to see her dodging streams of dark energy. Mateo stood next to her, trying unsuccessfully to break the energy stream.

"Jolene!" Eliza caught Jolene's attention and threw her her own amulet—the one Mariah Blackmoore had made.

Jolene caught the amulet easily and raised it toward the dark energy. Morgan watched, fascinated, as the energy hit the amulet, then clattered to the floor in a pile of black glass shards.

"Eliza! Over here!" Morgan gestured for her aunt to come over behind her where she could try to protect them both with the one amulet she had, but Eliza shook her head. She dived for the black glass shards. Dodging the brown energy streams of the guards, she ran toward Bly, lunged at him and shoved the shard into his eye.

Bly's screams sent a shiver down Morgan's spine and pulled the attention of the guards away. He covered his eye with one hand and pointed at Eliza who was making her way back to the girls with the other.

"Kill her!"

The guards trained their guns on Eliza, pummeling her with dark energy. Eliza's body jerked backward, almost as if on a pulley.

"No!" Morgan heard herself scream as Eliza stumbled backward toward the hole, perching on the edge for a split second before she toppled into it. Morgan couldn't stop herself from rushing over to the hole and looking down. Eliza's broken body lay on the rocks below. She didn't even have time to mourn—the guards were already turning their guns back on them. Morgan's eyes burned with tears as she tore herself away and raised her amulet.

Bly was clutching his eye and screaming orders at the guards. Morgan realized the guards were gaining ground—pushing them back toward the hole. Her heart squeezed—she hoped they wouldn't all end up meeting the same fate as Eliza.

Jolene took out another guard with one of her energy zaps. Mateo kept them at bay with constant rolls of energy waves. Celeste executed a few well-placed kicks. Fiona took out the last glowing crystal and held it up. Luke, Buzz, Cal and Jake kept trying with the Tasers.

At least we're able to keep Bly and his gang outside in the tunnel and they aren't pushing us further toward the hole, Morgan thought. But she knew the standstill couldn't last forever. Sooner or later, one of them would gain ground on the other.

A metallic sliding sound came from above and Morgan realized it was the round metal sewer cover moving aside.

What now? she thought, bracing herself for the onslaught of sewer water that would wash her five hundred feet to her death.

She glanced up, shocked when a face appeared looking down at them from up above. She felt the last spark of hope leach out of her. The face belonged to the last person she wanted to see—someone who would love watching their defeat at the hands of Bly.

Sheriff Overton.

Chapter Twenty-Eight

"Need some help?" Overton smirked at her, a toothpick bobbing up and down between his teeth.

"Not from you!" Morgan shouted up at him. Beside her, Jolene glanced up, a frown creasing her face when she realized who Morgan was talking to.

"Look out!" Morgan shrieked, pointing to a guard who decided to take advantage of Jolene's distraction by aiming at an unprotected blind spot with his dark energy gun. Jolene moved the amulet to protect herself while aiming a sizzling gold energy spark at the guard.

"I don't think you are in any position to argue," Overton pointed out. "I can get you out of here."

Morgan stared in wonder as a rope ladder dropped down from above them. Her eyes ping-ponged between Overton and the guards who seemed to have gained a few inches in the battle. Her sisters stole quick, nervous glances at her.

Looks like she'd have to choose between two evils. Her gut instinct told her to go up the rope, especially since it was looking like it was either that or die at the bottom of the hole.

"We have to go up!" Morgan yelled for the others' attention pointing at the rope.

They nodded, backing up while continuing to fight off the guards. Morgan didn't have to use her intuitive gifts to see this wasn't going to work. Once they took their attention away from fighting the guards to climb the rope, the guards would just rush right in.

As if reading her mind, Fiona raised her hand with the last red crystal.

"Looks like it's a good time to use this," she said, and launched it toward the opening.

Her aim was perfect. The energy knocked down the guards, but the best part was that it also dislodged the rocks from the top of the opening, temporarily closing it in.

"Let's go!" Morgan could hear the guards already trying to dig out the opening to get to them as Mateo scooped Johanna up in his arms and scurried up the ladder.

She shooed her sisters up and then Luke made her follow them before he, Buzz, Jake and Cal climbed up themselves, pulling the ladder up with them.

From the top, Morgan glanced through the hole to the rocks below, her heart twisting as she looked at what was left of Eliza, then Overton slid the cover back in place and they all stood there staring at each other.

Morgan glanced around the small room. Lengths of different sized pipes ran along the perimeter, leading out of the room at all angles. She guessed it was some sort of service room for the piping that fed into the facility up above.

Her gut flooded with a sense of urgency as she heard the guards yelling below. They must have broken through the debris caused by Fiona's crystal and were in the room. They wouldn't be able to climb up without a ladder, but surely, they would know another route to get to the room they were in. She guessed they didn't have long before Bly and his minions were breaking down the door.

Sheriff Overton looked different without his brown sheriff's uniform. He wore a stained white tee-shirt over tan slacks. The t-shirt was a little tight, bringing unwanted attention to his overstuffed belly. He hitched up his pants, switching the toothpick from one side of his mouth to the other.

"Well, I didn't expect to see you girls again so soon." His smug gaze drifted from one girl to another.

"What do you want?" Jake cut in. "I'm sure you didn't pull us out of there out of the kindness of your heart, so let's just get down to business."

"You always were uppity," Overton said to Jake. "But you're right. It seems like you have something I want and I have something you want.

"What could *you* possibly have that *we* want?" Jolene stood protectively in front of Johanna who leaned against Mateo on one side and a section of pipe on the other.

"I have a boat that can get you people out of here." Overton's lips curled in a mean smile and he nodded to a man who had been standing unobtrusively next to some sort of hatch. The man pushed the hatch open and Morgan leaned over to see a steep ramp leading down to a good-sized boat.

"We have our own boat," Morgan crossed her arms over her chest, "and rafts to take us to it."

"I don't think so." Overton pointed to another hatch, which was opened by another of his minions. Morgan's heart sank when she looked out to see the remains of their rafts deflated on the rocks.

"You didn't!"

Overton shrugged, switching the toothpick around in his mouth. "Better hurry up and make your decision. It won't take long for them to find us here."

Another explosion rocked the floor and Morgan thought she heard voices outside the room. Luke looked around at all of them, each giving a nod of the head.

"So, you'll take us to our boat?" Luke asked.

"Yep."

"And what do you want in return?" Fiona narrowed her eyes at Overton.

He leaned forward, his beady eyes drilling into hers. She shrank back as he reached toward her, grasping the meteorite locket in his hand and holding it up between them. "This fancy locket and asylum."

"Asylum? From what?" Luke asked.

Overton dropped the locket and stepped back. "I've been pursued by both sides of the paranormal community. Goldlinger is after me because of my little um ... indiscretion regarding your treasure and, well, you goodie-two-shoes people have always hated me."

"Hated *you*? You're the one that harassed *us*," Jolene said.

Overton shrugged. "That was just business. Anyway, obviously you girls have a lot of clout and now that you have your mother back, I want you to get the community to promise to protect me from Goldlinger and Bly."

Jake snorted. "It looks like you're in pretty good with them. After all, you are *inside* of Bly's complex. I think this is some sort of trick."

"Inside the underground sewer system—not the main complex." Overton spread his hands at his sides. "If Bly finds me in here, I'm as dead as you are."

Jake narrowed his eyes at Overton. "Then how did you get in in the first place?"

Overton smirked. "I still have my contacts in the organization and it turns out contacts will do lots of things for money. They got me in, but we better get out while the gettin's good."

Morgan stared at Overton, wondering where he'd gotten money to pay anyone off. Had he nabbed some of the treasure from their house? She didn't see how it was possible. For all she knew he'd never been inside, but maybe he'd been up to things she didn't know about.

"We aren't part of any community," Fiona said. "And even if we were, we certainly don't have any influence to get anyone to promise to protect you."

"I do." Mateo spoke from the corner where he'd been leaning against the pipes with Johanna. Everyone swiveled their heads to look at him.

"What are you talking about?" Jolene asked.

Mateo glanced uneasily out the door.

Were the guards out in the hall?

"I can explain later, but for now we need to hurry. I say we take him up on it." Mateo's face turned grim. "It looks like it's our only chance."

The girls glanced at each other, then at Johanna, who nodded.

"Okay, but I don't trust him." Fiona reluctantly handed the locket to Overton.

Overton took the locket with a smirk and nodded to the man, who opened the hatch.

"After you." Overton gestured toward the hatch.

Morgan still had her reservations. She hesitated, not sure if they should really trust Overton, but before she could think more about it, the sound of something heavy battering the door to the room jolted her into action. Mateo swooped Johanna up in his arms and they all ran for the boat.

It turned out that Overton could be trusted— at least long enough to take them to their boat that was waiting several miles away. Apparently, Bly had been too busy trying to put his eye back in the socket and never even suspected and they were able to make a clean get-away. Still, Morgan didn't let her guard down until they were all safely ensconced on the boat, watching Overton's boat disappear into the horizon.

"I can't believe he didn't double-cross us somehow," she murmured as she watched the moonlight dance across the tops of the waves from the cabin window.

"There's still time for that." Jolene slid along the bench seat to sit next to Johanna. Johanna looked tired. Morgan's heart pinched at how she'd aged, but when her mother looked up at her and smiled, warmth flooded her chest.

"He won't double-cross you. He needs you too much now." Mateo brushed his hand through his dark brown curls and Morgan's mind whirled with all the questions she wanted to ask. What was Mateo even doing there? What had happened to Jolene inside that compound? And last but not least, where in the world had her mother been all these years and why hadn't she contacted them?

Before she could ask any of the questions, Luke appeared in the doorway. He leaned against the doorjamb, his broad shoulders spanning most of the opening and asked the question for her.

"Does anyone want to tell us what the heck was going on in there?"

Epilogue

Jolene stood, hands on hips, in the east sitting room staring at the TV.

"*... In world news tonight, alternative energy expert Dr. Mortimer Bly's Caribbean compound on Fury Rock suffered massive explosions.*" The television screen flashed various aerial view pictures of damage to the research complex.

"*... Dr. Bly said the explosion was related to a new alternative energy he's researching.*" The television switched to a film clip of Bly talking. Jolene almost laughed when she saw the big patch on his eye.

"*... Bly himself was injured saving his research notes, but everyone else escaped with only minor injuries. He will rebuild and continue his research.*"

Jolene snapped the TV off and turned to face the others. "Can you believe that?"

"He has the perfect cover," Morgan said from her place on the couch in between Fiona and Celeste.

"The world will probably never know what his real motive is ... but we do," Johanna said softly from the overstuffed chair she'd been tucked into, a fuzzy white blanket wrapped around her despite the warm summer evening.

She was still weak, but managed a radiant smile as she sipped a cup of tea. Belladonna, who had ignored all four sisters and gone straight to

Johanna upon their arrival home, purred contentedly in her lap. In the two days that they'd had their mother home, she'd improved immensely. Her skin was losing its deathly pallor and she'd even been able to walk a few steps on her own without the wheelchair they'd rented to help her get around.

Would she ever get back to her old self?

Jolene had no idea, but it didn't matter. She was glad to have her mother back home in any capacity.

"I'm just glad we got out of there in one piece," Fiona said.

"Yeah, but I wonder about Overton. I still don't trust him and now he has that locket," Morgan said. "What do you think he plans to do with it?"

Jolene shrugged. "Who knows? Maybe build his own paranormal army."

"I hope not," Celeste said. "You guys never located the woman who brought it to your shop?"

Fiona shook her head. "Nope. I guess she's another mystery."

"Maybe she was part of this paranormal community and brought it to you on purpose," Celeste suggested.

"Maybe. I guess there was a lot going on in the paranormal community that no one told us about." Morgan bristled.

"Because you weren't ready," Mateo said.

"Actually, we didn't even know there *was* a paranormal community," Celeste chimed in.

"Yeah, but now I guess we're part of it ... whatever that means." Morgan pressed her lips together.

"And what do Dorian Hall and the government have to do with all this?" Fiona scrunched her face up at Luke.

Luke shrugged. "She's pretty tight-lipped, but the government has a vested interest in making sure Bly doesn't gain any more power. Apparently, she knew that you girls would eventually be able to help her. I think that's why she hired me—she knew I could get close to you because of my relationship with Morgan."

"So you didn't get fired?"

Luke laughed. "No. I kind of think she actually wanted us to go there, she just didn't want to give the order officially."

"You'd think she could have warned us before all of this started so we could have been honing our skills," Celeste said.

"You know the government. They like to keep people in the dark."

"That's for sure," Cal said and everyone chuckled.

Celeste turned to her younger sister. "Well, Jolene, it turned out your instincts about something not being right with the investigation into Mom's death was spot on."

"I'll say," Johanna chimed in, setting off another round of laughter.

Jolene's heart squeezed thinking about what her mother had suffered at the hands of Bly ... and she'd submitted to it in order to keep them safe. But she did feel a little bit of satisfaction in knowing that she'd been right to be suspicious about Johanna's death—Maybe Morgan wasn't the only one with intuitive gifts.

"Yep," she said. "Turns out that photo I found in Barnes' storage unit was actually a photo of Mom being grabbed from the cliff the day she supposedly died. She never jumped off—she was kidnapped—and they paid off Earl Whiting to say he saw her jump!"

"Wait." Celeste lifted a brow at her. "You went to the storage unit alone?"

Jolene grimaced. She hadn't told anyone about her trip to the storage unit and how she'd been attacked. "Yeah, I guess I probably shouldn't have done that. But at least I didn't get captured there."

"No, but you almost were," Mateo cut in.

Jolene blinked at him. "How'd you know that?"

"Who do you think got you out of it?" He winked at her.

"Oh." Jolene chewed her bottom lip. So she really *had* seen Mateo in town—he had been looking out for her after all.

"Thanks," she said. "I still don't get how they could have grabbed me, though. They used some kind of weird rock—it looked like a geode but it made me terribly weak. I couldn't fight back. And what happened to that picture, anyway?"

"The geode is something we need to be careful of. Bly had them specially fitted to sap all your energy. The problem is they're kind of bulky, so he can't use them everywhere. But, for trying to capture someone they work pretty well." Mateo turned to Jolene. "As you found out. As far as the picture goes, well … let's just say if one of those guys has it, he won't be showing it to anyone. Ever."

Morgan raised a brow at Mateo then looked down at the obsidian amulet. "I wonder if these amulets would counteract the geode?"

Mateo pressed his lips together. "I'm not sure. The amulets absorb energy, right?"

Morgan nodded.

"The geodes suck out energy, so the amulet probably wouldn't counteract them."

"Good point," Jolene said, then narrowed her eyes at Mateo. "So, if you stopped them from grabbing me at the storage unit, how come you let them grab me at the college?"

Mateo's eyes flashed. "I can't be everywhere. Watching over you is like a full time job. The day you were snatched, I was on Fury Rock with Bly. I'd infiltrated it about a year ago to try to get Johanna out, so I couldn't spend too much time away from there."

Johanna smiled at Mateo. "It made my life a lot easier."

Morgan turned to her mother. "Mom, I don't understand why you never contacted us."

Johanna's eyes clouded. "It tore me up not to, but I couldn't. It was too dangerous. I knew your gifts would get more powerful and I couldn't risk bringing Bly's attention to you. Once he kidnapped me, I realized it was better for you girls if I just submitted to what he wanted instead of fighting him off. Of course, little did I know he was already watching you, and when my power dried up, he came for you anyway. But by then I was too weak to fight."

Jolene's heart twisted and she shot Morgan an angry glance. "Of course you were, Mom. We know you did what you did for us."

"I did send one little message, though." Johanna reached into her pocket and took out two tiny heart shaped pictures ... the exact size of the locket Jolene wore on her neck.

Jolene gasped and her hands went up to the necklace. "You mean this really is your locket?"

Johanna nodded and Jolene remembered how Mateo had ripped it from her throat, and then how the mysterious black cat had returned it with the vial of the red liquid. She turned to Mateo. "You took the locket, but how did you—"

Mateo shook his head, cutting her off. "I have my ways."

"So, all that time he was draining your energy to make it into some kind of elixir that his minions would drink?" Jake asked Johanna.

"Yep. And that's what he had in store for Jolene, too."

"But now he has no one, or at least not that we know of," Mateo said.

"I guess that's one thing in our favor," Morgan added. "He won't be able to use any elixirs to boost the power of his underlings. And meanwhile *we're* getting stronger."

"But what about that guy Barnes?" Celeste asked. "Did his boat blowing up have anything to do with this?"

"As a matter of fact, it did. And it helped us solve a case," Jake answered. "Bly doesn't like to get his hands dirty, so it seems. He had a small time crook, Edwin James, grab Johanna from the cliff."

"That figures," Luke said. "Most of the big-wigs hire others to do the dirty work."

Jake nodded. "The Noquitt police brought James in and, my sources tell me, it was pretty easy to get him to spill his guts. Apparently, Barnes was out fishing the night Johanna got grabbed. He took the photo from his fishing boat and was blackmailing James with it. Poor Barnes only got one payment, though, before James killed him and dumped him in the ocean. His boat was supposed to be blown up back then, but somehow that didn't happen until James went back to cover his tracks recently.

Somehow, Barnes' bones made their way into Jeb's lobster traps. Jeb's cousin was actually the one to find them—he's kind of shady and has apparently been pilfering Jeb's traps for years. Except this time instead of lobsters, he got human bones! Word travels fast across the criminal element in this town and somehow James found out and went and cut the trap lines so no one would pull up more of Barnes' bones. Then he must have gone back and blown up the boat."

"But why go to all that trouble now?" Celeste asked. "That all happened seven years ago."

"Apparently, James was scared stiff of Bly finding out he screwed up by having a witness to Johanna's abduction and was afraid of what Bly would do to him if he found out. He was afraid Barnes' bones surfacing now would launch an investigation and it would all come out. That's why he talked to the police. He's so scared of Bly that he gave up the information as a trade for protection."

"And it almost worked," Cal said. "Except he missed one bone."

"Yep," Jake nodded. "The one Jeb found in his lobster trap."

"So the whole thing with his traps had nothing to do with Gordy Ellis and the feud?" Fiona asked.

"Nope, I already talked to them and they shook hands and buried the hatchet on that old family feud, hopefully for good."

"Wow, that's great news!"

"And I also solved another case, too." Jolene smiled. "That's why I was at the college. Gail was taking cooking lessons—not having an affair. She wanted it to be a surprise for Steve, which explains all the secrecy. She confessed and they're happier than two clams in a clamshell ... and eating much better, too."

Everyone laughed, then Celeste's face turned serious. She turned to Jolene.

"So, what exactly happened to you in Bly's compound?"

Jolene told them about her cell and how she thought Mateo was one of Bly's minions up until the very end. She described the chair and how Bly wanted to make the elixir from her paranormal powers. She left out the part about the black cat and her locket, but finished up by describing how Mateo had tricked Bly by monkeying with the chair so they could incapacitate Bly and grab Johanna to make their escape.

"... And that's when we met up with you guys in the tunnels," Jolene said to her sisters, then narrowed her eyes at Luke. "But where were *you* then? We only ran into Eliza, Morgan, Fiona and Celeste. You guys weren't there."

Luke told her about the energy shield and how they'd gotten separated. "We didn't know where the girls had gone so we figured the best way to find out was to get one of us captured and hope that Bly would lead us to you. Then the others would follow and jump out to help at the right time."

"Wow, that was pretty dangerous." Morgan's eyes softened as she looked at Luke. "You could have ended up like Eliza."

Jolene's heart pinched thinking about her aunt. "I wish we could have gotten to know her better."

"She was wonderful," Johanna said. "We were very close at one time. Everyone thought she left Noquitt because she was bored here, but that wasn't true. She had to leave because there was so much paranormal power here between your father, her and me, that it would have attracted a lot of attention. We felt it was safer for you girls if she left. She gave up her home and we should never forget that she did that for *us*."

Jolene ran over and hugged Johanna. "We won't, Mom. But I think I speak for everyone when I say the most important thing is that we have you home with us. Let's just chill out and enjoy that ... and work on getting you better."

"That would be lovely, dear," Johanna said. Her voice was light, but by the way she looked out the window toward the dark wooded area at the edge of their property, Jolene could tell her mother was wondering the same thing she was—how long would it be before Bly struck again.

***

The old woman stood just inside the thickly wooded edge of the Blackmoore property, looking toward the house, her face hidden by the wide hood of the black cloak she wore. At her feet, a jet-black cat with ice-blue eyes lazily washed its face.

From her vantage point, she could see the figures of the Blackmoore family and friends gathered in one room. Her keen ears could hear the murmur of conversation and occasional outburst of laughter but she couldn't make out the words that were being said.

A smile played along her lips as she watched from her hiding spot—all was at it should be ... at least for now.

She'd done her part and now, maybe, her weary old bones could rest. She turned and faded into the darkness of the woods, the cat following along closely behind her.

***

Ten days later ...

Jolene sat on the porch looking down at the lavender-colored envelope she held in her hands. It was addressed to her and her sisters and, even though it had no return address, she knew who it was from.

Tears stung the backs of her eyes as she rocked back and forth in the white wicker chair, taking care not to knock over the bottle of beer that sat next to her bare feet. A cool breeze fluttered across the back of her neck, giving her a moment of relief from the hot summer day.

She tapped the edge of the envelope against her lips.

Should she open it before her sisters came home?

Her curiosity won out. She slid a fingernail under the flap. The scent of lavender wafted out and she closed her eyes before taking out the neatly-penned letter. A single tear slid down her cheek as she read:

Dear Girls,

If you are reading this now, it means I'm dead. Please don't be sad, it was all for a good cause. Just know that I always loved you girls and that's why I did what I did. I'm sorry we won't get to know each other better, and even though we can't talk to one another, I'll still be around in spirit.

You girls have an important job ahead of you now. The future rests on your shoulders and you must pick up where I left off. Enclosed you will find a map that may aid you in beating Bly to one of the relics that he desperately desires.

It's up to you girls to carry on our cause,

Yours,

Eliza.

A piece of paper that had been folded up inside the letter fluttered to the ground and Jolene bent to pick it up. It was a map, but not of any place that she recognized. She turned it over but the other side was blank. Pressing her lips together, she re-read Eliza's letter. There was no indication what exactly it was a map *to*.

She sat back in the chair and took a sip of the beer. A purple dragonfly landed on the arm of her chair and she stared at it, mesmerized. She'd seen lots of dragonflies before, but never a purple one.

She sipped the beer and contemplated the map. She and her sisters would have to figure out what the map was for, of course. She wasn't about to let Bly get any of the relics he wanted.

With a sigh, she folded the letter back into the envelope and got up from the chair. Her sisters would be home in a few hours. She'd show the letter to them then. In the meantime, she'd get on the computer and see if she could figure out what that map was to—maybe by the time they got home she'd be able to give them a destination for their next adventure.

The End.

***

Want more Blackmoore Sister's adventures? Buy the rest of the books in the series:

Dead Wrong (Book 1)
Dead & Buried (Book 2)
Dead Tide (Book 3)
Buried Secrets (Book 4)

Sign up for my newsletter and find out how to get my latest releases at the lowest discount price:

http://www.leighanndobbs.com/newsletter

A Note From The Author

I hope you enjoyed reading this book as much as I enjoyed writing it. This is the fifth book in the Blackmoore sisters mystery series and I have a whole bunch more planned!

The setting for this book series is based on one of my favorite places in the world - Ogunquit Maine. Of course, I changed some of the geography around to suit my story, and changed the name of the town to Noquitt but the basics are there. Anyone familiar with Ogunquit will recognize some of the landmarks I have in the book.

The house the sisters live in sits at the very end of Perkins Cove and I was always fascinated with it as a kid. Of course, back then it was a mysterious, creepy old house that was privately owned and I was dying to go in there. I'm sure it must have had an attic stuffed full of antiques just like in the book!

Today, it's been all modernized and updated—I think you can even rent it out for a summer vacation. In the book the house looks different and it's also set high up on a cliff (you'll see why in a later book) where in real life it's not. I've also made the house much older to suit my story.

Also, if you like this book, you might like my Mystic Notch series which is set in the White Mountains of New Hampshire and filled with magic and cats. I have an excerpt from the first book "Ghostly Paws" at the end of this book.

This book has been through many edits with several people and even some software programs, but since nothing is infallible (even the software programs) you might catch a spelling error or mistake and, if you do, I sure would appreciate it if you let me know - you can contact me at *lee@leighanndobbs.com*.

Oh, and I love to connect with my readers so please do visit me on facebook at *http://www.facebook.com/leighanndobbsbooks* or at my website *http://www.leighanndobbs.com*.

Are you signed up to get notifications of my latest releases and special contests? Go to: *http://www.leighanndobbs.com/newsletter* and enter your email address to signup - I promise never to share it and I only send emails every couple of weeks so I won't fill up your inbox.

About The Author

Leighann Dobbs has had a passion for reading since she was old enough to hold a book, but she didn't put pen to paper until much later in life. After a twenty year career as a software engineer with a few side trips into selling antiques and making jewelry, she realized you can't make a living reading books, so she tried her hand at writing them and discovered she had a passion for that too! She lives in New Hampshire with her husband Bruce, their trusty Chihuahua mix Mojo and beautiful rescue cat, Kitty.

Find out about her latest books and how to get discounts on them by signing up at:

http://www.leighanndobbs.com/newsletter

Connect with Leighann on Facebook and Twitter

http://facebook.com/leighanndobbsbooks

http://twitter.com/leighanndobbs

More Books By Leighann Dobbs:
Mystic Notch
Cat Cozy Mystery Series
** * **

Ghostly Paws

Blackmoore Sisters
Cozy Mystery Series
** * **

Dead Wrong
Dead & Buried
Dead Tide
Buried Secrets

Lexy Baker
Cozy Mystery Series
** * **

Lexy Baker Cozy Mystery Series Boxed Set Vol 1
(Books 1-4)

Or buy the books separately:

Killer Cupcakes
Dying For Danish
Murder, Money and Marzipan
3 Bodies and a Biscotti
Brownies, Bodies & Bad Guys
Bake, Battle & Roll
Wedded Blintz
Scones, Skulls & Scams
Ice Cream Murder

Kate Diamond
Adventure/Suspense Series
* * *

Hidden Agemda

Dobbs "Fancytales"
Regency Romance Fairytales Series
* * *
Something In Red
Snow White and the Seven Rogues
Dancing On Glass
The Beast of Edenmaine
The Reluctant Princess
Sleeping Heiress

Contemporary
Romance
* * *

Sweet Escapes
Reluctant Romance

Excerpt From Ghostly Paws

In over thirty years as head librarian for the Mystic Notch Library, Lavinia Babbage had never once opened the doors before eight a.m.

I knew this because my bookstore sat across the street and three doors down from the library. Every day, I passed its darkened windows on my way to work. I watched Lavinia turn on the lights and open the doors every single morning at precisely eight a.m. from inside my shop.

Most days I didn't pay much attention to the library, though. It was really the last thing on my mind as I walked past, my mind set on sorting through a large box of books I'd purchased at an estate sale earlier in the week. The edges of my lips curled in a smile as I thought about the gold placard I'd had installed on the oak door of the old bookshop just the day before. *Wilhelmina Chance, Proprietor*. That made things official—the shop was mine and I was back in my hometown, Mystic Notch, to stay.

I hurried down the street, deep in my own thoughts. The early morning mist, which wrapped itself around our sleepy town in the White Mountains of New Hampshire, had caused the pain to flare in my leg, and I forced myself not to limp. I continued along, my head down and engrossed in my thoughts when I nearly tripped over something gray and furry. My cat, Pandora, had stopped short in front of me causing me to do a painful sidestep to avoid squashing her.

"Hey, what the heck?"

Pandora blinked her golden-green eyes at me and jerked her head toward the library ... or at least it seemed like she did. Cats didn't actually jerk their heads toward things, though, did they?

Of course they didn't.

I looked in the direction of the library anyway. That's when I noticed the beam of light spilling onto the granite steps from the half-open library door.

Which was odd, since it was only ten past seven.

My stomach started to feel queasy. Lavinia never opened up this early. Should I venture in to check it out? Maybe Lavinia had come in early to catch up on restocking the bookshelves before the library opened. But she never left the door open like that. She was as strict as a nun about keeping that door closed.

I stood on the sidewalk, staring at the medieval-looking stone library building, my pre-caffeine fog making it difficult for me to decide what to do.

Pandora had no such trouble deciding. She raced up the steps past me. With a flick of her gray tail, she darted toward the massive oak door, shooting a reproachful look at me over her shoulder before disappearing into the building.

I took a deep breath and followed her inside.

"Lavinia? You in here?" My words echoed inside the library as I pushed the heavy oak door open, its hinges groaning eerily. The library was as still as a morgue with only the sound of the grandfather clock marking time in the corner broke the silence.

"Lavinia? You okay?"

No one answered.

I crept past the old oak desk, stacked with books ready to return to the library shelves. The bronze bust of Franklin Pierce, fourteenth president of the United States, glared at me from the end of the hall. I didn't have a good feeling about this.

"Meow." The sound came from the back corner where the stone steps lead to the lower level. Dammit! I'd warned Lavinia about those steps. They were steep and she wasn't that steady on her feet anymore.

I headed toward the back, my heart sinking as I noticed Lavinia's cane lying at the top of the stairs.

"Lavinia?" Rounding the corner, my stomach dropped when I saw a crumpled heap at the bottom of the stairs ... Lavinia.

I raced down the steps two at a time, my heart pounding as I took in the scene. Blood on the steps. Lavinia laying there, blood in her gray hair. She'd fallen and taken it hard on the way down. But she could still be alive.

I bent down beside her, taking her wrist between my fingers and checking for a pulse.

Lavinia's head tilted at a strange angle. Her glassy eyes stared toward the room where she kept new book arrivals before cataloguing them. I dropped her wrist, ending my search for a pulse.

Lavinia Babbage had stamped her last library book.

***

I called my sister Augusta, or Gus as I called her, who also happened to be the sheriff, and sat on the steps to wait. I might have drifted off, still sleepy from the lack of caffeine, because the next thing I heard was Augusta's voice in my ear.

"Willa, are you okay?"

I opened one eye to the welcome sight of the steaming Styrofoam coffee cup that Gus was holding out to me.

"I'm fine," I said, reaching for the cup.

"What happened?" I studied Gus who stood on the steps in front of me. No one would have guessed we were sisters. She was petite, her long, straight blonde hair tied back in a ponytail, which, I assume, she thought made her look more sheriff-like. Even in the un-flattering sheriff's uniform, you could tell she had an almost perfect hourglass figure. I was tall with thick wavy red hair, my figure more rounded—voluptuous, as some described me. The only thing we had in common was our amber colored eyes—same as our mom's.

"I was on my way to open the bookstore when I noticed the lights on in the library." I glanced down the street toward the municipal parking lot.

Now that the spring warm-up was here, I was trying to work in some extra exercise by parking in the lot two blocks away instead of on the street near the bookstore.

"Was that unusual?" Gus asked.

"Yep." I looked over my shoulder at the front door of the library. "It sure was. Lavinia never opens the library before eight. Plus the front door was cracked open, and she never leaves it open."

Gus started up the steps toward the library. "Did you touch anything?"

I stood up, wincing at the pain in my left leg—a reminder of the near fatal accident over a year ago that was one of the catalysts for my move back to Mystic Notch. The accident had left me with a slight limp, a bunch of scars and a few odd side effects I didn't like to dwell on.

"Nope, other than Lavinia. I didn't know if she was alive and needed aid," I said as I followed Gus into the library.

Gus stopped just inside the door and looked around. The coppery smell of blood tinged the air, making me lose interest in my coffee.

"It doesn't seem like anything is out of place ... no sign of struggle," she said.

"Nope, I think she just fell down the stairs." I started toward the back. "You know she was getting on in years and not that steady on her feet."

We turned the corner and my stomach clenched at the sight of Lavinia at the bottom of the steps.

"That's her cane?" Gus pointed to the purple metal cane, which was still lying as I'd found it.

"Yep. Looks like she lost her balance, dropped the cane, and fell."

Gus descended the stairs, her eyes carefully taking in every detail. She knelt beside Lavinia, studying her head. "She's pretty banged up."

"I know. These stairs are hard stone. I guess they can do a number on you." I winced as I looked at the bloody edges of the steps.

"So, you think this was an accident?"

"Sure. I mean, what else could have happened?"

"Yeah, you're probably right. No reason to suspect foul play." Gus stood and looked back up the stairs, down the hall and then back at Lavinia.

Her lips were pressed in a thin line and I wondered what she was thinking. I knew she was a good cop, but the truth was I didn't really know her all that well. Eight years separated us and she was just a teenager when I'd moved down south. Now, twenty-five years later, we were just becoming acquainted as adults.

"Mew." Pandora sat on the empty table in the storage room where Lavinia temporarily stored new books or returns before she catalogued them. I'd forgotten she was here. She wasn't really my cat ... well, not until recently. I'd inherited her along with the bookstore and my grandmother's house. I still wasn't used to being followed around by a feline.

"Isn't that Pandora?" Gus asked. Gus had been close to grandma—closer than I had, and it was somewhat of a mystery that Grandma had left me the shop, her house and the cat. In her will, she'd said she'd wanted me to come back home and have a house and business, which was odd because the timing had been perfect. She'd left a tidy sum of money for Gus, so at least there were no hard feelings.

"Yeah, she rides to work with me."

Gus raised a brow at me, but didn't say anything. Pandora stared at us—her intelligent, greenish-gold eyes contrasting eerily with her sleek gray fur.

"So, if it was unusual for Lavinia to be here at this time of the morning, why do you think she was here and what do you think she was doing?" Gus asked.

"I'm not sure."

Gus reached out to pet Pandora, who still sat on the table staring at us. "Are there any mice in here, Pandora? Maybe Lavinia heard something down here and wanted to investigate."

"Maybe." I looked around the floor for evidence of mice. Lavinia ran a pretty tight ship so I doubted there would be any mice in the library. And, since the room was empty of books, she hadn't come in early to catalogue new arrivals.

Which begged the question ... why *was* Lavinia in the library this early in the first place?